MY LIVING NIGHTMARE
AND OTHER STORIES

Bharti Patel

MINERVA PRESS

LONDON
ATLANTA MONTREUX SYDNEY

MY LIVING NIGHTMARE AND OTHER STORIES
Copyright © Bharti Patel 1998

ISBN 0 75410 444 3

First Published 1998 by
MINERVA PRESS
Sixth Floor
Canberra House
315–317 Regent Street
London W1R 7YB

Printed in Great Britain for Minerva Press

MY LIVING NIGHTMARE
AND OTHER STORIES

I would like to dedicate this book to my children,
Misty, James, Umesh, Dipak, Dimple
and especially Amit,
to my sister Amita, my niece Alisha
and my nephew Sunny,
for their devoted help in my writing these stories.

Contents

Croft   9

Return to Cinders   22

Trojan, the Tin Man   36

Champagne   52

Autobiography of a Potato Crisp   54

My Living Nightmare   56

Betrayal   58

An Ace, the Winning Card   61

One Day in the Life of a One Pound Coin   64

Adventures of a Carrot   66

Prem Nivas, the House of Love   68

A Statue   71

The Spirit of Christina   73

Rose Princess   97

Croft

After hearing about Scotland, the Highlands and open fields, all her life, Rose was at last going to live in that country. For the last eighteen years, since she was one, she had heard a lot about Scotland where her father grew up. It had not been possible before for Rose to go although her father did visit the place every six months to keep up with the estate business.

Her parents, Jim and Mary, met at a Christmas party in the orphanage called Hollyoaks. Mary was left abandoned outside Hollyoaks one night, twenty-five years ago. The owner, Mrs Holly Brown, now a widow, didn't have any children of her own, so, when her husband died suddenly of a heart attack at the age of forty-five, she decided to turn her house into an orphanage. She had plenty of maternal love to give and the only way she could do that was to give it to children who had no one.

Mary loved Mrs Brown very much, and because of that she did not leave Hollyoaks as others did when she turned eighteen. She decided to stay behind and help Mrs Brown run the orphanage.

One Christmas party Mary was playing blind man's buff with the children when Jim walked in through the door. He had just come from the airport, having flown down from Scotland. He just stood there holding his suitcase, fascinated by this young woman who was clearly enjoying herself. She had a blindfold on her eyes and was trying very hard to catch the children running around her. Jim saw her come towards him but did not move away. And then she was holding on to him and at the same time removing her blindfold. They both fell in love the instant their eyes met.

'Jim, I see you have met Mary,' said Mrs Brown, coming from the kitchen.

'Mary, this is Jim, my nephew,' she said, turning to Mary.

They just looked at each other without saying anything. Mrs Brown was so pleased. She knew they were made for one another when she invited Jim to come and visit her. She just wanted to see their reaction. Now that she had seen them both together, she knew she had done the right thing in inviting Jim. They were married in the new year. Mary did not want to leave Mrs Brown alone so Jim decided to conduct his business from Hollyoaks and left his manager to run his estates, called Glen Acres, in Scotland.

His parents had passed away within a year of each other five years before, and as he was an only child, Jim had nothing to stop him from moving.

Soon after, life returned to normal in Hollyoaks for Mary, except that she was now married to Jim and enjoying the married life. Their love for each other grew stronger as time went by.

Two years after they were married, Mary gave birth to a beautiful daughter. They named her Rose. Rose was loved by everyone. She was just like Mary in nature – loving and very kind-hearted. Rose grew up to be just like her mother and Mrs Brown, helping and looking after orphaned children.

One morning, Rose took up the breakfast tray to Mrs Brown as usual. Rose had taken it upon herself to give Mrs Brown breakfast every morning after she had become ill with flu a week before. Rose tried to wake Mrs Brown. When, after several attempts, she would not wake up, Rose checked her pulse. Mrs Brown had passed away peacefully in her sleep. Everyone grieved for her, Mary especially because to her Mrs Brown was like the mother she never had.

Now that Mrs Brown was gone there nothing to keep Jim there. He decided that it was time for them all to return to Scotland. After talking about it to Mary and Rose, he left Hollyoaks in the capable hands of a loving couple, Mr and Mrs Smith. Making sure that the Smiths had settled in properly and were going to run Hollyoaks the same way that Mrs Brown ran it, Jim left Hollyoaks with Mary and Rose to go to Scotland.

The flight to Edinburgh did not take long. Their driver, David, from Glen Acres, was waiting for them at the airport to take them to their home.

Rose found the scenery so fascinating, a complete contrast to London. Here all she could see was hills and fields covered with green grass; in some places cattle and sheep grazed in the green fields.

Jim had told them that Glen Acres was on the outskirts, about five miles away from a town called Cumbernauld. Even though Mary had grown up at Hollyoaks and had only been to Glen Acres a few times with Jim, she always found the peace and quiet of the place overwhelming. It felt like coming home after a hectic day at work.

Suddenly Rose started feeling an uneasy tingling of dread, as if something horrible was going to happen. She felt as if she had been there before. The scenery looked familiar to her. She knew she had never been to Scotland before now, so why this familiarity? She thought it might be because her father had spoken so much about Scotland, and especially Glen Acres and his business, that she felt as if she already knew the place.

David drove the car right up to the front of the big white house. It was a detached house with five bedrooms and a double garage attached beside it. The front of the house was surrounded by rose bushes which were well kept and trimmed. Almost all the colours and types of roses could be seen while Rose was still in the car. She quickly leapt out and ran up to take a good look at the flowers and the surrounding fields. The fresh air and clear skies were a complete contrast to London which was always filled with polluted air and noisy with the constant flow of the traffic. Rose liked Hollyoaks but she fell in love with Glen Acres as soon as she saw it. She told her parents that she was going to explore the back of the house.

'You must be tired after your journey. At least have a little rest before you go exploring. You'll have plenty of time later to do that,' Mary told Rose while helping Jim with some of the smaller luggage from the car, but Rose could not be restrained.

'Just half an hour, Mum. I don't feel too tired,' said Rose, touching and smelling a beautiful red rose, and then going to the back of the house without waiting to hear what her mum had to say.

Jim just laughed and told Mary he was glad Rose liked the place. 'It will make it easier for her to settle down here.'

Just as Rose rounded the corner of the garage she saw a man coming towards the house from the fields. His head was down so he did not see Rose as she stood transfixed, staring at the man. As the man neared Rose he became aware of someone watching him. He looked up and the shock of seeing a young girl standing by the garage was so great that he too stood transfixed, staring at the girl.

'Victoria.'

'Father.'

They both spoke at the same time. Rose started feeling that dread of doom, everything started jumbling in her mind and even before he reached her, she felt herself falling.

★

Victoria Brown was over the moon. Tomorrow was her eighteenth birthday and her father, John Brown, was giving a lavish party. He was also going to announce her engagement to Byron. Dear Byron, only a year older than Victoria but very mature for his age; he was the local laird's son, and Victoria's father was the manager of their estates. Victoria had known Byron since childhood; they had grown up together, gone to school together. As Victoria's childhood blossomed to adulthood so their love for each other blossomed.

Mr Brown and the laird, Mr George Macmillan, already knew about their children's feelings for each other. Mr Macmillan had always treated John Brown more as a friend than his manager. Both of them had agreed to announce their children's engagement on Victoria's eighteenth birthday.

After tossing and turning for what seemed to be most of the night, Victoria fell into a deep sleep only to be woken up late by a beautiful sun shining through her bedroom windows. Her bedroom was full of flowers, all of them roses. She loved roses. There was a big birthday card propped against her dressing table and a well-wrapped present just beside it. She quickly got up and went to the card. It was from her father. Then she opened the present. In it was the most beautiful, green chiffon dress Victoria had ever seen. When she took out the dress, a piece of paper fell down. She picked it up and read the message on it.

To the most beautiful daughter,

This dress belonged to your mother. She wore it on her eighteenth birthday and I would like you to wear it tonight.

Love,
Father

Victoria was overwhelmed by the gesture for she knew that even now her father treasured all her mother's belongings. She wished her mother were alive today. She died when Victoria was born, so Victoria had never seen her, but her father gave her all the love she needed, being like a father and mother to her.

Byron took her to lunch in the afternoon and while at the restaurant he gave Victoria a beautiful locket with a chain. When Victoria opened the locket, it had miniature photos of herself and Byron it. For the second time during that day Victoria had tears in her eyes. They were tears of joy, first for her father's gift and now for Byron's gift. They both spent the afternoon roaming the shops for engagement rings and then the countryside on a nice long walk.

Byron left Victoria at her home at around five o'clock promising to be there by eight before all the guests arrived. Mr Brown was busy organising the party in the barn. She did not want to disturb him so she went to her room instead to have a nice long soak in a bath and get ready for the party. She was just emptying her bag when she realised that Byron had left behind the shirt and tie he had bought earlier on. These were the clothes that he wanted to wear later so Victoria decided that she would get ready quickly and then go to Byron with his clothes. They could come back together.

By half past six she was ready. The dress fitted her perfectly. Victoria put on the chain and locket which Byron had given her. It looked beautiful. After applying a little make-up she was ready. Putting a light shawl around her shoulders she left to go to Byron's place. Her father was still busy so she knew that he wouldn't even know that she was gone. Anyway, she would soon be back with Byron.

When Victoria reached Byron's house she went straight to his room, but he was nowhere to be found. She decided he might be at the croft at the back of the house, so she went there. By now it had started raining so as soon as she arrived she flung her shawl on a nearby chair and went to the fireplace, which was lit, to warm herself because by now she was shivering from the rain. She called out to Byron but no one answered. She was just wondering where else Byron could be when she heard a noise behind her.

Mr Macmillan stood by the door looking at a half-drowned girl. He had been drinking since early afternoon. He was very fond of his drink. That was his only weakness. Byron had told him not to drink too much today but Mr Macmillan couldn't resist one small glass of whisky. Then one led to another and before he knew it the bottle was half empty. He was sitting in the study in the croft enjoying his drink when he heard someone call out. He stood up and went to see who it was. What he saw was a beautiful girl in a green chiffon dress who was trying to warm herself by the fire. Something in Mr Macmillan's drugged mind snapped and he was filled with lust for this girl, and he started approaching her, lust in his eyes.

Victoria turned around to see Mr Macmillan by the door. She was just about to ask him where Byron was when she sensed a change in him. He was coming towards her with a strange look in his eyes. It made Victoria frightened of him.

All Mr Macmillan wanted at that moment was to make love to this beautiful young girl. He took hold of her and started kissing her. The more the girl started struggling the stronger he became. When she tried to scream he put his hand on her mouth to stop her from screaming out loud.

He tore her dress and other items of her clothing with his other hand. With one hand still on her mouth he raped her.

Afterwards, when he removed his hand from her mouth, he saw that she just looked at him. She did not even flicker her eyelids. Mr Macmillan, having come to his senses, realised he had not just raped a girl but had also killed her by not knowing that when he had placed his hand on her mouth it also covered her nose and so had cut off her air supply. Not only that but the girl turned out to be not just anybody but his son Byron's future intended.

'Oh God, what have I done?' he cried in despair.

He knew he couldn't tell Byron about this so to hide his secret guilt he took Victoria's body into the loft of the croft and boarded it up.

*

When Rose came round she was lying on a couch with her mum and dad looking very worried. There was also another young man in the room. He was introduced to Rose as Dr King.

'You worried us, Rose. You fainted outside the garage. My manager, John Brown, brought you in. When you did not come round after a few minutes, we got worried and called Dr King. He came as soon as possible,' Rose's mum said worriedly.

'How long have I been out?' asked Rose.

'Nearly half an hour,' replied the doctor, coming over to check her pulse.

'Dad, I had a weird dream,' said Rose, trying to sit up. 'It felt so real.'

'It's only a dream. Don't worry about it, darling. But

what happened to you out there? Why did you faint? If it had not been for John, we would not have found you until late,' said Rose's mum, still looking at her worriedly.

Rose was the first person to see John Brown enter the room. She just looked at him then said, 'It wasn't a dream, was it? It really was true. Why do I get the feeling that I know you very well? And why do I get the urge to call you my father?' asked Rose, sitting up. 'You took much older than I remember.'

John Brown came near her. He sat down beside her, took hold of her hand and said, 'I knew you would come back, Victoria.'

On hearing this, Rose fainted again. Seeing the condition of his daughter, Jim took John to one side and asked him what the hell was happening between him and his daughter. John went to Rose to make sure that she was all right. After getting an assurance from Dr King that she was okay he told them to sit down, for what he had to tell them would take a long time.

John told them everything about his daughter, Victoria, who looked exactly like Rose, from the time she was born till the time she suddenly disappeared on her birthday. Since then he had been looking for her everywhere. In the end he had given up his search and at last settled down again as manager hoping that one day his beloved Victoria would turn up and say why she went away the way she did.

So engrossed were they all in listening to John that no one had realised that Rose was conscious again and had heard most of the story. She also knew that she had been Victoria in a previous life, and that John Brown was her father. What she thought was a dream was actually true and had really taken place in a previous life.

'Father.'

At the sound from the couch both Jim and John turned around at the same tune to go to her. After a little deliberation John let Jim go to Rose. Rose took hold of his hand and said that what John had told them was true.

'I remember being Victoria. I feel as if all I remembered actually happened in this life.'

She looked at John and said, 'I know you were my father. You still are my father. But now this is my dad,' she said, looking at Jim. She turned back to John and went on, 'I know how you must feel. I did not run away as you all think. Only I know what happened to me, Father,' said Rose. 'How could I leave you all when I was very happy with you and Byron? What happened to Byron? Where is he?'

John came to sit beside the other side of the couch, took hold of her other hand and replied, 'Byron is still alive. He never married after you disappeared. He still blames himself for your disappearance. He cannot figure out why you did it, but reckons it must have been his fault'.

'But Father, I did not run away,' said Rose.

Then she told them all about her dream. When she finished she noticed that the room was totally silent. In the end Jim said, 'I don't believe a word of what is being said but I know my Rose would never lie. The only way to find out if this is all true is to go to this croft.'

Rose wanted to go straight away but was also frightened of what they might or might not find there.

Dr King wanted Rose to rest for a few days but knowing that the mystery of her dream had to be found, she could not be restrained. In the end they decided to go to the croft the following day. As it was, the croft was about fifty miles away and by the time they arrived it would be late at night, so it was decided that they would leave in the morning.

That night Rose had the same dream again. She woke up feeling very nervous, not knowing what the day would bring. Jim decided to take Dr King with them in case something happened to Rose again and Mary also wanted to go, so the five of them left at around eleven o'clock to go to the croft. The journey took them an hour. Jim stopped the car outside the house. They all got out of the car and started to mount the stairs to the house but Rose went around the house in the direction of the croft. She felt a kind of pull towards the croft.

Byron was just coming out of the croft when he saw a young girl walking towards him. He couldn't believe it. It was Victoria, his Victoria. She hadn't changed one bit even after all these years. Soon his surprise turned to anger. How dare she come back after nearly twenty years!

'What do you want now? Haven't you done enough damage? How dare you show your face after all this time!' he said angrily as he came towards Rose.

'I'm sorry, Byron, but I am not who you think I am,' said Rose, a little frightened. She had never met Byron in this life but she felt as if she had loved him all her life and felt that love stronger now than ever. He looked older than she remembered. Gone were his boyish features which were now replaced by strong, manly ones, but she still loved him.

John reached them as Rose said this. Before Byron could say or do anything, he took him away to tell him what Rose had told them, leaving her alone with her parents and Dr King.

Rose took them inside the croft as if she knew the place inside out. Again she told them exactly where and what had taken place. By the time she reached the loft, she was shivering very badly. By that time Byron and John had also joined them. Byron moved up to Rose and gathered her close. He could feel her shivers right through him. Rose felt as if she had come home in his arms. It felt so right. Pointing to the far side of the wall, Rose said, 'I was buried behind those boards.'

Jim, John and Dr King went to open up the boards.

After quite a struggle they were loosened and removed. What they saw behind the boards shocked them all. There was a skeleton in there which fell out as soon as the boards were removed. The skeleton was wearing a chain with a locket. Jim picked it up and opened the locket and with his own eyes he saw the miniature pictures of Rose and Byron when he was young.

Up until that moment he had still had his doubts about the whole affair but after seeing the pictures in the locket he too could not deny the truth. John just knelt over the skeleton and started crying. Rose, who had felt dreadful up until now, stopped shivering and went to John.

'Victoria might be dead for you, but I have come back as Rose, Father. Please accept me as your Victoria. At last you have found me,' said Rose, as she too knelt beside him.

'Oh darling, you really have come back. Thank God,' said John, still crying and hugging Rose at the same time. Byron was so angry about the turn of events, and that Victoria had died, that he immediately left the loft to go to the house to see his father. No wonder he never came to the croft anymore. Come to think of it, his father had never once gone to the croft since Victoria's disappearance. Now he understood why he felt closer to Victoria in the croft than in the house and why his father had started drinking even more since that awful day and always stayed drunk. At the time Byron had thought that his father was unhappy for him and so had started drinking a lot.

Byron went straight to his father's room.

'How could you do that, Father? How could you?' he said, going to his father.

'What are you talking about, Byron?' asked Mr Macmillan.

'As if you don't know what I am talking about. You know damn well I am talking about Victoria,' replied Byron, standing over his drunkard father with hatred in his eyes. 'I could kill you with my bare hands, Father. We have just found Victoria's body in the loft of the croft. How could you?' he asked again in anguish.

'How did you find out?' asked Mr Macmillan.

'Would you believe it if I told you it was from Victoria herself?'

Just as Byron said this, Rose walked into the room with her parents, John and Dr King.

Mr Macmillan collapsed as soon as he saw Rose and died there and then from a massive heart attack. Rose went to Byron and took hold of his hand. 'I'm back, Byron. I still love you,' she said.

'I love you too, Victoria. I never stopped loving you,' he said, then laughed and asked, 'What shall I call you: Rose or Victoria?'

Return to Cinders

After marrying her Prince Charming, Cinderella thought all her troubles were over and that now she could put all that unpleasantness behind her and be happy ever after with her Prince. She was no longer Cinderella, but rather Ella to her Prince. Little did she know that her stepmother and stepsisters, Esmerelda and Griselda, although they presented a happy front, were still as jealous as ever of her good fortune.

After her marriage to the Prince, Ella, feeling sorry for her stepmother and stepsisters, took them to stay with her at the palace. They were given the whole of the top floor of the west wing in the palace. They were also given the freedom of running the wing the way they wanted. Ella never interfered with them but made sure they were always happy. She never thought of them as stepmother and stepsisters; to her they were her real family.

One day, the Prince had to go to their neighbouring country on some urgent business. The King would have gone but as he was not feeling well, the Prince decided to go on his behalf. He did not want to leave Ella behind but as the matter was urgent, he had no choice but to go. Before he went he told her to look after herself and said that he would try to be back as soon as possible.

Two days after the Prince left, a messenger brought a message for Ella, which said,

Darling Ella,

I will be arriving by noon. Please meet me at the lake. Also bring a picnic basket with you. Intend to spend whole afternoon with you alone.

All my love,
Prince

Ella was so happy. Even though they had been apart for only a few days, she missed him very much. At about half past eleven, Ella left the castle to meet her Prince by the lake with the picnic basket. The lake was situated behind the castle beyond the gardens. It was secluded by the trees. Ella reached the lake with ten minutes to spare, so she sat down by the tree. Resting her back on the trunk, she was soon lost in her own private thoughts. So deep in thought was she, that she did not hear anyone approaching. By the time she sensed that someone was beside her, it was too late. Before she could turn around she felt a sharp pain at the back of her head. The last thing Ella remembered was being carried by someone and then she lost consciousness.

When Ella came around she was lying on a bed. The room was in darkness. She tried to get up but her head hurt too much so she gave up the effort of getting up. She must have fallen asleep again, because when she opened her eyes again it was daylight. This time her head did not hurt her as much when she stood up. She was in a room with a single bed in one corner. There was a fireplace in the opposite wall. Two cooking pots, a couple of plates, mugs and a box of food were placed by the fireplace. A small table and two chairs were placed by the window near the bed. On the table was a small bag. When Ella opened the bag, she saw that it contained a few of her clothes. Ella could not understand how she came to be in this room. She went outside and stood there looking around her in horror. The 'room' was in fact a small hut with no other rooms and was surrounded by trees. By the look of the small vegetable garden she reckoned someone else must be living here.

Taking a chance, she walked through the trees. It did not take her long to find out that she was on a small island which was situated in the middle of nowhere. All around the island was water with no other islands or any landmark in sight; there wasn't even a small boat. She could not see any other person around. She realised she was all alone on this island and stranded. Ella went back to the hut. She couldn't understand why anyone would leave her all alone here. She thought she must have been kidnapped and was being held on the island for ransom.

Ella was hungry. She could not remember when she had last eaten. She did not even know how long she had been knocked out. There was a small bump at the back of her head which still hurt. She went through the box of food. It contained some biscuits, dried fish, dried beans, vegetables, fruit and preserves in jars. She took some dried beans and vegetables out of the box, put them in the pot half full of water, which Ella had got earlier from the stream beside the hut. Next she built a fire with the wood she found outside, heated the soup in the pot and ate it. Ella felt better with the food inside her. Afterwards she went to the bag on the table to take out a change of clothes. She decided to take a bath in the lake she had seen just beyond the hut. As she took out a dress from the bag, a letter fell out. Ella opened it and was shocked at the contents of the letter. It read:

At last our revenge is taken. You thought that your marrying the Prince and giving us a place to stay in the palace would be enough. We do not want charity from you. By right the Prince should have married either me or Griselda, not you. Even Mother agrees with us, so we made a plan to get rid of

*you. Now you are where you belong. You will never be able
to get out from that place. No one knows the place except us
and you can be certain that we will not tell anyone of your
whereabouts. Soon the Prince will forget you and marry one
of us. At last we will have what was rightfully ours. By the
way, I have also put your precious glass slippers in the bag.
We do not want the Prince to have anything to remember
you by. The sooner he forgets you, the quicker he will marry
again.*

Esmerelda

As written in the note Ella found the glass slippers at the
bottom of the bag. Now Ella knew why she was on the
island. She made a vow that no matter how long it took she
would get out of this place and punish them for what they
had done to her. She would not be lenient with them
anymore and would have them banished from the country
for ever.

Ella started filling her time by getting the vegetable garden sorted. She tried to chop down a tree to make a raft but
felt too weak and as it was a hot summer it tired her very
quickly. Ella knew it would take her a long time to build a
raft but she was determined that no matter how long it
took, she would succeed in the end, and she also knew that
her Prince would be looking for her. She was sure that if
she did not get off the island soon at least her Prince might
find her and rescue her.

One day, a week later, Ella woke up feeling very sick.
The sickness stayed with her almost every day. She thought
it must be the dried food she was eating from the box so
she changed to eating only vegetables and fish, if she
managed to catch one, but even that did not help. Suddenly
it clicked that she might be pregnant, because she started
taking a fondness to eating only certain foods. She had

heard from the cook in the palace kitchen, talking about such things, that her daughter was pregnant and she had a craving for certain foods.

Time soon passed by, and Ella started feeling different. Her stomach was swelling a little and all she wanted to do was eat her favourite food and sleep. She knew that now she would not be able to make that raft and get off the island before the baby was born so she left it up to her Prince to find her and settled down to looking after herself and the child she was carrying. She could just visualise how happy he would be to see his child as well as her.

The Prince came back a week after Ella was kidnapped from the lake. On his way back all he could think about was how much he had been looking forward to seeing Ella again. He missed her very much. The past nine days without her had been very lonely. He had left the neighbouring country as soon as he was able, but even then it seemed too long. He couldn't wait to tell Ella how much he loved and missed her. As soon as the Prince reached the castle he went looking for her in their suite. When he couldn't find her there he searched everywhere, even the gardens and the lake, with no joy. Thinking she might be in the kitchen helping the cook, as she sometimes did, the Prince went there. He asked the cook, who replied, 'I thought Ella was with you this past week.'

When asked why she thought that, the cook replied, 'Ella told me she had received a message from you telling her to meet you at the lake at noon with a picnic basket. When neither of you came back, the King and all of us took it for granted that everything had gone well and that the two of you had decided to spend a few days away by yourselves.'

'But I have just arrived today and I did not send any message,' said the Prince.

He became very worried. He asked everyone including

Ella's stepmother and stepsisters, but they all said that no one had seen her. He asked his guards to start a search for her. Everyone in the country started looking for Ella for she had been very kind to them and they all loved her. There was no ransom note so the Prince knew that she had not been kidnapped. He himself went to search for her all over the country but did not find her. He came back to the palace after being away for months looking for Ella. All he did was sit by the lake and drink. He lost interest in his country. The King, seeing his son unhappy and losing interest in everything, took over.

Months became a year and still the Prince did not come out of his depression. He could not forget Ella, not knowing how or where she was. His heart told him that she was still alive so, if she was not kidnapped then why didn't she come back to him? Not only had she disappeared without a word to anyone but she had also taken her glass slippers with her because the glass cage that stood in the gardens, and in which the slippers were kept, was empty and broken.

He was sure someone must know something but no amount of reward brought any news of her. The King tried his best to get the Prince occupied in some of the projects, but even that did not work.

Three years had passed since Ella's disappearance before the Prince, coming to terms with Ella not coming back, started taking interest again in helping his father with the running of the country. Everyone was happy to see their Prince coming out of his depression. They all still missed Ella with her smiling face but no one had yet managed to find her whereabouts. It seemed as if she had just disappeared from the face of the earth with no traces left behind her.

Seeing the Prince in a better mood Ella's stepmother decided now was the time for Esmerelda to start flirting with the Prince and get him to fall in love with her. The

Prince had been very kind in letting them stay on and because they treated him well and sympathised with him, he had no reason to doubt them, plus he thought they had changed for good. The Prince told Esmerelda that he was not interested in anyone when she started showing an interest in him. Still she did not give up hope, believing that sooner or later the Prince would marry her. Little did she know that the Prince saw them as sisters, as he told his father one evening when the question of his marrying again had cropped up and his father had told him that, if he wanted, he could marry either of Ella's two stepsisters. The Prince had replied that he saw them as sisters and as it was he was in no mood to get married again.

Seven years had gone by since Ella's disappearance when the Prince at last agreed to marry Princess Maria from a neighbouring country to strengthen the alliances between the two countries for he knew now that Ella was not coming back, ever.

On hearing the news of the Prince's engagement to Princess Maria, Esmerelda and Griselda became very angry. They knew life would not be same when the Prince married again. Their future in the palace became very insecure. They did not know what to do so, to bring Ella back from the island, if she were still alive after all this time, would be a bigger disaster for all three of them since the Prince would definitely banish them from the country for ever if he ever found out that they were responsible for her disappearance. They would just have to be in the Prince's good books if they were to continue to stay here.

★

The first year for Ella on the island had been very harsh. What with her expecting, her health had been in a poor state for the first few months. No matter how she felt, she got up and looked after her vegetable patch, for she knew that there wouldn't be anything else to eat if she did not look after it. She wanted to live for her Prince and her unborn child, and for that she would have to keep her energy up and wits about her. She made the hut as comfortable as possible and spent her time either going for long walks or growing wild flowers outside the hut which she found on her walks. In the long winter evenings she stayed inside the hut and from one of her few dresses she made little outfits for her unborn child. Ella had found a few blankets and bedsheets under the bed. She made a small hammock for the baby with one of the blankets.

Her son William was born just as winter was turning to spring and as there were a few daffodils just beginning to bloom. William was such a beautiful baby. He had the Prince's blue eyes and Ella's black hair. She cried the day he was born for the loss of her Prince and also for him not knowing that he had a beautiful son.

William grew up to be a very loving child. When he was six years old Ella thought the time was right for William to know his true identity so she told him everything; from the time of her father dying, her stepmother and stepsisters' treatment of her, how the fairy godmother had helped her to go to the ball, falling in love with the Prince, marrying him and her stepsisters' hand in her being left on this island to fend for herself.

William was a very intelligent boy for his age and he said, 'Mother, where is the fairy godmother? Why isn't she helping you get off this island?'

'I don't know,' said Ella, 'I have prayed that she would come to rescue me but I have not seen her since I married your father. I wish she would come and help us.'

'Mother, now that I am old enough, I will help you build that raft and we will leave this place as soon as it is ready,' said William bravely.

Ella thought that even for his age William spoke like an adult. She was so proud of him.

After that they both would go to the jungle and with William's help Ella started building the raft which had never been built in the first place. Even with William's help, it took Ella a long time to chop down a few thin trees and then to cut them into right sizes for the raft. By now the weather was getting warmer.

One evening Ella was in the garden tending to her flowers when suddenly her fairy godmother appeared from out of nowhere. Ella was taken aback at her sudden appearance. She asked her fairy godmother where she had been all this time when she, Ella, had needed her.

'I was away at the other side of the world helping others. On returning, I noticed that everybody in the country was celebrating. I became an ordinary person and asked someone the occasion for this celebration. That's when I found out that the Prince is getting married the day after tomorrow and that you had disappeared seven years ago. I am sorry that I neglected you. When I left you were very happy with your Prince and I thought my work here was done. I should have known better,' said the fairy godmother.

Ella couldn't believe that her Prince was getting married. She told the fairy godmother that the Prince could not marry again for now he had a son. Even if he did not want Ella back, he should at least accept his son. Then she took the fairy godmother inside the hut and showed William to her. The fairy had tears in her eyes as she watched the sleeping boy. When they were outside again, she told Ella again how sorry she was to have neglected her in the time of her need, but now she would help her.

She told Ella that everything would be fine and that the castle was about fifty miles south, and then she disappeared. She wished she could do more to help Ella and her son, but they were given only limited powers to help their godchildren. She wished she could transport them both to the castle just by waving her wand but that was not allowed. They were allowed to help up to a certain limit.

After breakfast next morning, Ella and William went to the shore where they had left their half-built raft. In its place stood a boat with a boatman. Ella told William that her fairy godmother had appeared last night, but she did not tell him about his father's impending wedding.

The fairy godmother had changed the raft into a boat and a frog she had found nearby into the boatman the previous evening. The boatman told Ella he was waiting to take them ashore. Ella went back to the hut and collected a few items. She said a silent goodbye to the island as they were moving away in the boat. William could not wait to meet his father. If her Prince did not want her then Ella had decided that she would just leave William with him and go back to the island where she had spent the last seven years, but William had a right to be with his father as well as to the throne which would be his when he was old enough. If she told William all this she knew that he would not leave her but she could not deny her son his rights.

They reached the mainland early next morning. Ella thanked the boatman and started towards the church. The fairy godmother had told her where the wedding was taking place. When they turned around to give a final wave to the boatman he had disappeared and so had the boat.

Ella covered her head and part of her face with her shawl for now there were a few people out and about. She did not want anyone to recognise her. By the time they reached the church she reckoned she was too late, for the church was filled with people. So were the grounds nearby, with the citizens of the country. They had come to see their loving Prince getting married at last. They had seen his unhappiness and despair when Ella had gone missing. At last he was to find the happiness he craved.

Ella thought she had lost her Prince by the look of the crowded church and celebrating citizens. She did not want to see him with another woman. She decided to leave William at the church and go back to her island to spend the rest of her remaining days of her life. She told William to go inside and seek the Prince, and then tell him that he was Ella's son, but he should only tell this to the Prince and no one else because if her stepmother and stepsisters were there they would not let him see the Prince at all.

Then from the folds of her shawl Ella took a package which contained the glass slippers and gave it to William. She told him only to give the package to the Prince, and no one else, as it was the proof that William was his son.

When William asked her to go in with him, Ella said that as she was not dressed nicely like other people present in the church, she would wait for them both out there. As soon as William went into the church Ella left to go back to the island.

William went into the church a little hesitantly for this was the first time in his life he had seen so many people, and all of them were dressed so very nicely. Some of them turned around to look at him. His clothes were very old so they reckoned he must belong to someone outside. They asked him to go to his parents but William said that he must see the Prince for he had a message just for him. Knowing how the Prince loved his people they pointed him out to William and allowed him to go forward. When William reached the Prince he tugged at his coat.

Sensing someone tugging at his coat, the Prince looked around. He saw a little boy of about five or six years old. He bent down to this little boy. He felt a kind of a pull just looking at him, as if he knew this boy, but how could he when this was the first time he had set his eyes on this child? The Prince bent down to ask him his name and if he wanted anything.

'William,' replied the boy, at the same time giving the package to the Prince. 'I am Ella's son. She has sent me to speak to you. She is waiting outside.'

On hearing this, the Prince quickly opened the package to reveal the glass slippers, which were without doubt his Ella's. How could he have forgotten them? He quickly dashed outside with William, leaving behind him people with stunned expressions. He asked William where Ella was. William told him that she was just by the doors when he came in, but now she was nowhere in sight. The King soon joined the Prince and so did Princess Maria. The Prince introduced them to William. The King was pleased to meet his grandson. The Prince was still looking into the crowd outside, hoping to see his beloved Ella.

Sensing the Prince's inner turmoil and knowing that he still loved Ella, Princess Maria said to him, 'Go find your wife. I release you from all commitments.'

The Prince was very happy and said he was glad to know that she understood him and would always be her best friend. He asked William where he thought Ella might have gone to. William said that he did not know but only that morning, they had come ashore by a boat. The Prince asked him which way they had come.

William pointed out the way. The King told his son he would look after William and get to know him while he was to get Ella back. Leaving William with his father, the Prince mounted his horse and went in the direction William had pointed out. On the way, the Prince passed an old woman covered from head to toe. He passed her by but something about her made him stop and look back at her. It was the way she was walking, for he remembered Ella's walk very well after all these years. The Prince went back to her.

Ella had seen someone pass her on a horse and when he turned back she realised it was her Prince, but he no longer belonged to her for he was married. So as not to be recognised Ella pulled her shawl over her head and her face more closely, leaving only the eyes. When the Prince came near her and got off the horse, she just stood there saying nothing. The Prince said, 'Ella, I don't care why you left me all those years ago, but now that you are back why just leave our son with me and walk away? I want to know what I was supposed to have done wrong. I love you even now and want you beside me as my wife.'

Knowing that the Prince did not know the circumstances behind her disappearance she told him everything and as proof showed him the letter which she had taken on leaving the island. Then she said, 'But I cannot come back now that you have married again. You do not need me. I only came back to bring your son to you. I'm going back to my island.'

The Prince told her that the wedding was off. He wanted her, his Ella, beside him and no one else. Ella was so happy. She fell happily into her loving husband's arms. In that moment she forgot about the misery of the past seven years. They sat down on the grass nearby and talked for a long time. They talked about their past, present and future plans.

On reaching the palace they both were received by everyone in great jubilation. The guards were told to arrest Ella's stepmother and stepsisters who were then taken to the dungeons. The country celebrated well into the night. Prince William was the toast of the town.

A week after their arrival the Prince, Ella, a few guards and Ella's stepmother and stepsisters went to the island. He saw where his beloved wife had spent the past seven years and this made him very angry and depressed because while he was staying at the palace in luxury, his Ella was staying in the worst conditions all alone, and also with no one to help her in her hour of need at the birth of their son. He had tears in his eyes but Ella told him not be unhappy for this time they were going to be together for ever.

No matter how much Ella's stepmother and stepsisters pleaded with them, they were left behind on the island as they had left Ella. The Prince told them that he was going to make sure they never left the island alive. They were to spend the rest of their lives there alone, and that he himself would make sure that they stayed on the island. With those parting words the Prince, Ella and the guards left. Ella never saw them again and also gave a silent prayer to her fairy godmother thanking her yet again for bringing them all back together.

Trojan, the Tin Man

Roger Brown always believed himself to be lucky; what with loving parents, Richard and Ruth, and his sister Rachel who, although two years younger than him, had watched over him since the age of ten when Roger nearly drowned in the small pond in their garden. She was more like a friend to him than a sister. Roger could tell her anything and knew she would always keep it to herself. If he ever needed a friend to talk to, Rachel would be the first person Roger would turn to. His parents were happy in the knowledge that Roger and Rachel would always have each other to turn to if anything should happen to them.

They lived in a six-bedroomed house situated in South-gate, in a quiet residential area. A short driveway with beautifully kept lawns surrounded by rose bushes led to the house. The front door opened into a big hall which had three exits, one of which led to a big, family-sized kitchen off which patio doors led to a big garden. This too had well-maintained lawns which were also surrounded by different coloured rose bushes. In the middle of the garden stood a man-made pond with a fountain in the centre. Two reception rooms, a bar and library were situated off the kitchen. The other exit in the hall led to Rachel's bedroom. This was originally a dining room which led to a day room. The minute Rachel saw it, she fell in love with it and no amount of her parents' persuasion to take a bedroom upstairs would change her mind so they had the connecting wall from dining room to day room removed and installed a fitted bathroom for Rachel. The third exit in the hall was an alcove which had a staircase leading straight up to a landing which contained five bedrooms. All of them had their own bathrooms. The windows were replaced by French windows which opened on to a balcony that continued right round the house. The main bedroom was occupied by Roger's parents, another by Roger himself and the other three were turned into guest rooms.

They were very wealthy. Roger's mum enjoyed just being a housewife and mother. Mr Brown's business, Beltamore, which produced their own leather and metal belts and unusually shaped buckles for the belts, was doing very well in Luton. At the moment Mr Brown ran the business with his brother George who ran the buying department. He wanted Roger to take over from him when he graduated from college. Roger wanted that too, but not yet. He wanted to travel around and to see something of the world before he took over the reins of Beltamore. Roger told Rachel of his plans. She agreed with him but realised that he couldn't do anything about it. She knew that they both loved their parents very much and wouldn't do anything to upset them.

So, after getting his diploma Roger joined his father's firm at the age of twenty-five. He put his dreams of travelling on hold for the time being and gave one hundred per cent of his dedication to his work at Beltamore.

Within two years, seeing how dedicated Roger was to his work, Mr Brown semi-retired and gave his chair to Roger. Now he only came to the offices twice a week. Rachel too decided to join the firm and soon became Roger's right-hand person.

Roger and Rachel loved creating new designs for belts and buckles. Rachel was very artistic so she was always coming up with new and unusual designs on buckles. On

Roger's twenty-seventh birthday, she gave him a silver buckle with a star engraved into it. Roger loved it very much and always wore it.

One evening, Roger received a phone call from the police. Beltamore was on fire. By the time Roger, Rachel and Mr Brown reached the place the fire had been put out. Everyone did what they could to salvage most of the goods. The ground floor, where most of the goods were, was in ruins. There were water and ashes everywhere and the place was still filled with smoke. The whole place was damaged beyond recognition, but miraculously the upstairs offices had been saved. The fire had not reached them so, except for smoke, there was no damage there. Soon everyone went home. Rachel tried to get Roger to leave everything until morning but he was very adamant about not leaving the place. He was upset and trying to figure out how the fire had started because he was very particular and careful about all the electrical appliances. Rachel left with Mr Brown, leaving Roger alone.

Roger was aimlessly walking around among the ruined goods when suddenly there was a big thunderous noise followed by lightning. Roger went to the open window to look out. He was standing by the window when there was a flash across the sky. This time the lightning struck Roger straight in his midriff. Roger felt the impact as it struck his belt buckle. The last thing he remembered was flying across the room and hitting something very hard before everything went blank.

When Roger came to it was dark. He tried to focus to see where he was but the effort was too much and he ached all over. He must have fallen asleep because when he opened his eyes again it was to bright daylight. He realised now that he was in a hospital bed. His parents and Rachel were in the room. They were so happy to see him awake. Before he could ask how he came to be in the hospital

Rachel said that she had been very worried about leaving him alone at Beltamore so after dropping their dad back home, she went back to be with him. She found him unconscious and called the ambulance and had been with him since then, as had their parents.

Rachel told him that he was very lucky to be alive after being struck by lightning. He'd suffered a few broken ribs, shock and a mild concussion. Roger wanted to go home that very day but the doctors wanted to keep him under observation for another day because of the concussion. The following day, Rachel took Roger home. After resting throughout the day he had a nice long soothing bath before he changed into a grey polo-necked long-sleeved jumper and grey pants. He was coming down the stairs when Rachel walked in through the front door. She thought her brother looked handsome and walked with a grace of a panther. Roger had always maintained his physique. He worked out at least three times a week at a local gym and was a regular early morning jogger. Looking at him now no one would think that he had just come out of the hospital. Seeing him dressed all in grey, she had an idea. She went into her room and took out the belt with the silver buckle which she had given to Roger on his birthday. She had brought his clothes from the hospital and just left them in her room before helping Roger upstairs that morning. She gave Roger the belt. Roger thought how uncanny it was that Rachel gave him the belt now, just when he was thinking about it. As soon as he put the belt on, he felt a kind of electric sensation go through him like an energy. Roger didn't think much about it at the time and concluded that he must still be suffering from shock.

Roger spent part of the evening talking with Rachel and their father. They were still trying to figure out how the fire started and what to do next. Roger wanted to go to the factory but his father would not listen and told Roger to take a few days off to get better.

When Roger woke up the following day, he felt much better. His ribs were not hurting at all and there were no aches and pains in his body at all. He was very surprised. He told Rachel about it and she too was very surprised, but she was not taking any chances so she took Roger to the hospital to have him checked up properly. After x-rays and a check-up, the doctor confirmed that he did not know what caused it, but Roger's broken ribs had healed very well indeed. It was incredible to believe that just a few days ago Roger had been brought in with broken ribs and concussion because now there were no signs of any damage or bruises on his body. The doctor believed in miracles but not to this extent. Rachel brought Roger home. For once both of them were quiet and baffled. They did not know what to say to each other. On Roger's insistence Rachel did not say anything to their parents. Roger couldn't understand why but he wanted to keep this knowledge just between the two of them.

The following day, after assuring his parents that he would take things easy at work, Roger left with Rachel in the morning. On seeing the condition of the production floors and warehouse, Roger became very upset and angry as well. He phoned the police to see if they had managed to find out how the fire had started. Deep down Roger knew that even though he did not have any enemies the fire had been started deliberately by someone with a grudge for he had always been very careful about the safety of the goods and machinery. The police confirmed that it was arson and asked Roger if he had any enemies in the business. Roger said no, but that he would not rest until he found out the person or persons behind it. After the conversation with the police, Roger told Rachel what the police had told him. Neither of them could figure out who could have a grudge against them. They were doing very well in the business, their products were number one in the market, but they couldn't think of anyone they might have offended.

Cleaning up and reopening the factory took a couple of weeks. The damage was not as huge as had at first been predicted. The workers were very helpful and glad that they still had jobs. They did everything they could to make things better and more secure than before. Everyone was given an extra bonus for their devotion.

In the meantime Roger started feeling and noticing changes in his body. He became stronger. Lifting heavy weights was no problem to him. The first time he experienced this was when he was on the factory floor while they were cleaning up the mess made by the fire. Everyone was at lunch. Rachel was upstairs in office. Roger tried to move a heavy piece of machinery and was very surprised when he moved it as if it did not weigh more than a few pounds. It confused him and he thought that it must be a mistake or that he was hallucinating, so he tried again and again. After that incident Roger experimented on many things but only when he was alone: He found he could run and swim faster; he could read a book in no time; his hearing became very powerful for he could hear a person whispering next door; he could see very clearly in the dark; but most of all he found out that if he wanted to do something all he had to do was think and concentrate on it, such as moving something without even touching it. He could only do these things when he wore his favourite belt because when he removed the belt nothing happened. So the power was in the belt.

Two days before reopening Beltamore, Roger called Rachel into his room and asked her that if he said or did anything, would she keep it to herself. At first Rachel didn't know what Roger was talking about and nothing he said made any sense, but she loved her brother and knew that whatever he was talking about must be very important to him; so she agreed.

What she saw Roger do astounded her. He also told her the secret of the belt. Then Roger told her that he now remembered that the lightning had struck the buckle of the belt he was wearing before he was flung across the room and injured. Rachel still could not believe that the belt was giving Roger all these powers. She wanted to find out whether it was the belt or the buckle which had the powers so she told Roger to change the buckle of the belt he was wearing with another one. Roger tried the belt with another buckle but nothing happened. He tried wearing the belt without the buckle, and still nothing happened. Next he tried his buckle with another belt and felt the change in him instantly. So now they both knew that it was indeed the buckle which was giving Roger the power. The lightning must have transferred some kind of force when it struck the buckle. Now they both knew that it was the power in the buckle which had cured Roger so quickly as well.

Rachel was so excited that she wanted to celebrate by taking Roger out for a meal. She told him to dress up as she was going to take him to a very posh restaurant. Roger decided to wear a particular suit. No sooner had his mind been made up than he had the suit on him. Rachel saw this and it frightened her but Roger told her not to worry. This was the first time his power had changed his clothes. He didn't know what else was in store for him. He told Rachel that he was going to take one day at a time and try to adjust to the changes which were occurring in his life.

The opening of Beltamore went very well and soon work resumed as normal, but now Roger was very alert to everything that went on in the factory. Whoever it was might strike again.

A week after the opening, Roger was with Rachel in their office discussing the new line in leather when Roger heard muffled voices in the office down the corridor. What attracted Roger's attention was the way the conversation was conducted, a heated one but in very low tones. Roger put his mind to listening to the conversation. It took him a few moments to realise who one of the voices belonged to. He figured there were no more than two people as he did not hear anyone else talking. The voice he recognised belonged to his uncle George, but the other one he had never heard before. This person was demanding that a payment of twenty thousand pounds be paid to him straight away, saying that he had been told he would get paid as soon as the job was done and that was nearly a month ago. Uncle George said that he would have the money ready by the following evening and arranged a meeting place.

Rachel realised that Roger was not paying any attention to what she was saying. She asked Roger if anything was wrong but he just said that he had other things on his mind and was sorry for not listening to her. Rachel left it at that. She knew her brother well enough not to question him further. If he wanted her to know he would let her know in good time.

Roger was very restless that evening. He was trying to figure out why his uncle owed so much money to this man. He hoped his uncle was not in any trouble. He knew about his uncle's weakness for women. He reckoned this man might be blackmailing his uncle. Roger loved his uncle and wanted to help, but as he did not want his uncle to know that he knew, Roger decided to go and meet the man himself. Roger knew it was no use talking to his uncle as he would deny everything. Even though he was a friendly person, Uncle George always kept himself apart from all the family gatherings, saying that after his wife Maria died, his happiness died with her. Outwardly he led a decent life, as his son Jonathan was a very well-known lawyer.

In the end, Roger decided to confront the man demanding the money. Even though Roger had not seen him, he would definitely recognise his voice. He would try to get him before Uncle George. If not, he would confront him after the money was handed over and his uncle had left the area. Roger knew that if he confronted the man as himself, he might be recognised and would not get the right answers. He would have to disguise himself and try to be at the appointed place before his uncle arrived.

Now the problem was to find the right disguise. Recently, Roger had been thinking of putting his newly found powers to good use. He reckoned he was given these powers for a reason but he knew that he would not get any peace and quiet if he used them in public, so a disguise was a must. In his mind, he conjured up a lot of different outfits but nothing seemed to work. Roger stared at his buckle for a long moment trying to see if the buckle would give him a clue and finally an idea materialised. Why not dress himself in a monochrome outfit. With his mind set on an outfit such as his grey polo jumper and close fitting trousers, he changed himself into these clothes. The effect of them on him was electrifying, but his face was still exposed so Roger had his face covered with the same material of the suit except for his eyes, nostrils and mouth. Looking in the mirror, Roger couldn't even recognise himself. He was a completely changed person. He also changed the colour of his shoes to grey. Now even Rachel would not recognise him. He intended to tell her, he thought, but not until after the outcome of tomorrow evening.

The following evening, Roger reached the place before the time of the arranged meeting. It was very secluded and deserted at this time of evening. Nearly fifteen minutes elapsed without anyone passing by. Then a man dressed in a long overcoat passed Roger and sat down on a bench twenty yards away from where Roger was hiding behind the bushes. Now that it came down to the crunch, Roger was in a dilemma. He did not know how to approach the man. He wasn't even sure if this was the right person. If Roger approached the man as he was, he might be recognised and the man might flee the place. If he approached the man in his monochrome suit, he might take fright and could end up having a heart attack.

Luckily, the decision was made for him. The man took out his mobile phone from his pocket, dialled a number and started talking in a quiet voice. Even at this distance Roger recognised his voice as the one belonging to the other man in his uncle's office. Roger also found out the man's name was Patrick because the first words he uttered were, 'George, it's Patrick and I am waiting.'

Roger changed into his disguise and as Patrick was putting the phone away in his pocket Roger was already lifting him bodily from the bench and with a speed that left Patrick gasping, Roger took him about half a mile away from the bench. Roger asked why he was demanding so much money from George. At first Patrick did not answer, but when threatened with physical harm, and because Roger had frightened him, and also because Patrick did not know who this person was, who appeared to be in some sort of metal suit, he told this 'tin man' everything. Roger was very upset when he found out that his uncle had agreed to pay this man twenty thousand pounds for burning the place down and putting Beltamore out of business.

Roger took Patrick to the nearest police station and told him to confess to his crime or else he would find him, no matter where he went. Patrick asked this tin man what his name was. Roger said the first thing that came to his mind: Trojan. He left Patrick outside the police station and very quickly disappeared, but not before making sure that Patrick went inside to make his confession.

Next morning, the police arrived at the house and asked to speak to Mr Richard Brown. They all gathered in the living room before the police said that George had been arrested the previous night in connection with the fire at Beltamore. The police said that what baffled them most was that a man called Patrick gave himself up the previous night but insisted to the police that he was brought to the police station by a tin man who called himself Trojan. The policeman said that never in his life had he heard anything so stupid. Rachel looked at Roger who just winked at her. She knew it had to be Roger who took that man to the police station in his disguise but also knew that Roger would tell her all about it in his own time and when they were alone.

Roger went with his father to the police station. That was when he found out in his uncle's own words why he had the factory burnt down. Apparently, George was promised by his brother Richard that Beltamore would be half his when Richard retired but instead of doing anything about it, the running of Beltamore was given to Roger and Rachel, while he was left where he was and had been since the start of the business. On top of it all there was another company who had promised George a good share in their firm if Beltamore went down. So instead of being a dogsbody all his life, George agreed to take the stake in this other company and hired someone to set fire to Beltamore.

Roger couldn't believe his ears when he heard this. He told his uncle that if only he had come to him in the first place he would have found that thirty-five per cent of Beltamore was indeed in Uncle George's name. Uncle George was very ashamed of what he had done. Jonathan was also present as he was going to represent his father in this case. Both Jonathan and Roger tried to get him released but to no avail as he was the instigator of the fire.

As Roger and his father were leaving the room where Uncle George was held, they came face to face with Patrick who was handcuffed and on his way to the interview room.

He came over to where Roger and his father were and told them that the police did not believe him but that he was definitely brought to the police station by Trojan, the tin man.

As Patrick was led away to be interviewed, Roger left with his father. He dropped his father at home and went to the factory where Roger found Rachel waiting for him eager for him to tell her everything. As it was nearly lunchtime Roger took Rachel for a long drive. On the way out they bought sandwiches and coffee from a nearby bakery. While having their lunch in the car, Roger told Rachel everything that had happened from listening to their uncle's conversation with Patrick until leaving Patrick outside the police station.

A week after the incident, Uncle George received a sentence of six months despite the fact that Mr Brown did not press the charges against him since he had admitted that he had hired Patrick to set fire to Beltamore, and his sentence was light compared to Patrick's who was sentenced to one year's imprisonment. Jonathan was ever so grateful for his uncle's and Roger's support in all this. He said that he would always be in debt to them and would always be there for them.

Nearly two weeks after that Roger had to become Trojan again. Beltamore was once more running smoothly. The agency had sent them a highly recommended young man call Jack to fill their uncle's vacant position. Jack did his work with dedication and Roger was very happy with his work.

One sunny day in late July, Roger and Rachel were in the warehouse inspecting the quality of the belts which had just been packed – they often did spot checks on the goods themselves – when they heard that a special steam train designed to run on these tracks and travelling from Birmingham to London was out of control. This train did special outings for the local public twice a week to London and back again. It had not stopped at the last three stations and would soon be passing Luton. At the speed it was travelling, it would not be long before it entered London. It was reported by some eyewitnesses that the driver of the train seemed to be slumped into his eat. Disaster on a major scale was imminent if it was not stopped soon. Around one hundred and fifty to two hundred people's lives were in jeopardy. The main control room was trying to keep all the tracks on which the train was travelling clear, but no one could say how long it would be before there was a disaster of some kind. The radio announcer was saying that only a miracle would stop this disaster. At first Rachel was very shaken but soon she recovered, took Roger back to their office, closed the door and told him that he should do something.

Roger was very confused and said, 'Rachel, I don't think I can do anything. What if something went wrong or someone recognises me?'

But Rachel would not hear of it. She said, 'Roger, you are the only one who can help all these people. You have the strength, the speed and the power. Please at least try, otherwise you will regret it for the rest of your life.'

The few minutes it took Roger to make up his mind seemed like ages. Rachel had already switched on the television in their office, so Roger knew roughly where the train was at that moment, how fast it was travelling and also that the police and ambulances were on standby. The progress of the train was now being filmed by the TV crew travelling in their helicopter. Roger knew he could not waste any time now. Those people's lives might be depending on him. Rachel went with Roger to the rear of the factory. To anyone watching, it seemed as if the boss and his sister were inspecting the premises. Once out of sight and in a secluded place, even before Rachel could say good luck to him, Roger had already changed into his outfit and was away like a flash. By now Roger had gained more insight into his powers. If he put his mind to it his speed was faster than a fast car travelling in the fast lane at high speed. Not wanting to draw any attention towards himself Roger soon took to running on the underground track going in the direction the runaway train was travelling.

The train stations which Roger passed briefly were packed with people. Anyone who saw Roger passing through the stations was at first stunned to see what they thought to be a man dressed in grey running on the tracks. Soon they started telling others what they thought they saw. Some believed them and others did not.

Soon Roger was catching up with the train. One of the media men in the helicopter saw something grey moving at a fast pace. He nudged his colleague with the camera who was recording the progress of the train, and told him to zoom his camera on to this. He saw that it was a man covered completely in what looked like silver who was running very fast after the train. By now all the TV channels were broadcasting the runaway train followed by a grey man on the tracks. Rachel too saw this and prayed that Roger would be in time to save all those people on the train.

Ignorant of the sensation he was causing, Roger soon caught up with the train. He caught hold of the steel ladders on the rear of the train, climbed up them and started running towards the driver's compartment. He could hear people crying and screaming within the compartments. He could hear panic in their voices. Roger reached the driver's compartment and lowered himself into it through the window. There he saw the driver lying on the floor. The first thing Roger did was quickly look at the panels and switches and then he quickly got the train under control, slowed it and then stopped it. Then Roger checked the driver's pulse. It was there but very faint. He reckoned it was either an electric shock of some kind or that he might have suffered a heart attack.

Knowing now that the commuters in the train were safe, and would soon be rescued by the police, Roger carried the driver out of the train. He thought that if he waited for the ambulance to arrive the driver might not have a good enough chance to survive so he picked up the driver and quickly carried him to the hospital. Roger left him in the capable hands of the emergency doctors. When asked by one of the stunned doctors who he was, Roger replied, 'My name is Trojan. I am sorry I cannot stay and answer your questions.' With that he left the hospital.

In no time at all Roger entered the premises of Beltamore through the front entrance and went up to his office. He had already changed back in a quiet spot after leaving the hospital. From there he took a cab and went to the factory.

Rachel was waiting for him. Roger could see from her face that she already knew that those people on the train were safe. She took him to where the TV was still on and that is where Roger saw himself as Trojan. Roger couldn't believe that he was on TV. It looked nothing like him. It seemed as if Roger was seeing someone else and not himself on TV. The only thing Rachel did at that moment was give Roger a hug and a kiss, and said, 'Thank God there are no casualties.' She couldn't say or do anything at that moment as Jack had just come into the office also talking about this mysterious person who had single-handedly stopped the train.

On reaching home that evening, the first thing both Roger and Rachel saw was a photograph of Roger as Trojan on the front pages of the *Evening Standard*. Its headline read TROJAN, THE TIN MAN COMES TO THE RESCUE. Below the photograph was an account of the rescue as seen from the helicopter. There was an interview with the doctor who spoke to Roger, saying that the tin man had called himself Trojan and also about how the driver might not have survived if Trojan had not taken him to the hospital and instead waited for the ambulance to arrive as he indeed had suffered a heart attack and was now recovering in their intensive care unit. The papers also wanted to know who this Trojan was, where he came from, how he got there. They also wanted to know why no one knew about him, and that if anyone knew anything about him or his whereabouts, that they should come forward.

Champagne

My parent, the vine, was planted in the vineyard in the South of France in January. I was born in May with a lot of my brothers and sisters in one big bunch. Like us there were a lot of other bunches on my parent-vine. I was very happy with my brothers and sisters who kept me company all the time and we always played with each.

The time passed very quickly and in September we were picked from my parent-vine and put into big baskets. We were all nearly the same size and a beautiful shade of green. From there we were taken to a big warehouse. There for the first time I was separated from my family. It felt very odd because I felt very alone but soon I made some friends in the tub which we were put into. It felt very nice when I was washed and transferred to another big tub.

Then I was trampled by many feet for a long time until I shed my skin and became just the juice. My skin was left behind when I was strained in a big strainer and put into barrels. I was then taken to a cold storage room and was left there for a few months to ferment. During this time someone always came to check my progress.

It was February before I was transferred into a green bottle. I was shut in the bottle with a white cork and put into a big rack with little holes. The place was not warm, but it was not too cold either. I stayed there for a good few years before I was taken out of the rack. Champagne was the name I was given and the company put their label on me – Moët et Chandon. Being cooped up in the storage for so long made me very alcoholic. Seventeen per cent of me was pure alcohol. Anyone who was to drink a couple of glasses of me would get slightly drunk.

I was sold to a very big chain of supermarkets by the name of Tesco. There I was put on the shelf to be sold again.

One day, a very good-looking couple came and bought me. As they had just got engaged they wanted to celebrate with me and caviar. I was the toast of this important occasion. And what a way to go as well.

Autobiography of a Potato Crisp

I was born in a field in Cornwall. My parents had beautiful red skin. I grew up with my brothers and sisters. We were kept underground to grow fully.

As spring turned to summer I wondered when it would be my turn to come out of the ground. I was dying to see the outside world. I had heard a lot about it from my parents; what it felt like to have sunshine upon you and the difference in weather too because when you are underground you don't feel anything except the warmth of the earth.

At last the day came when I felt the earth tremble and I knew that the farmer had come to take us out of the ground. We were dug up at about eleven in the morning. It was a wonderful feeling to have beautiful sunshine on your face – so nice, and a different kind of warmth. Together with my brothers and sisters we were put in a big tank where we were washed. I was separated from my family in the process. After that we were put to dry a little and then packed in cardboard boxes and put on a truck.

We were taken to a factory where again we were washed and scrubbed of any dirty marks. I was put into an electric machine which sliced me into thin slices. I was then sprinkled with salt. Everything happened so quickly. I did not even have time to look around me except to glimpse big tanks and machines and to hear a lot of noise. After a fifteen minutes' soak in salt I was put into a big fryer where I was fried until I turned out nice and crispy.

I was taken out of the fryer and put in a big tray to cool down. After I had cooled down I was taken and packed in a small bag. What a lovely bag it was too. Nice and silvery inside to keep my flavours intact, and painted red outside. Red's always been my favourite colour, and as soon as I was put in it and sealed I felt very proud of myself.

For you see, not only did I end up in my favourite colour but I was bought by a very well-known company, 'Walkers'. I was packed with other crisp packets in a box and am waiting at the moment on a shelf at Sainsbury's for someone to buy me and take me home.

My Living Nightmare

One night my parents went to a celebration party and, as I was not feeling well, I stayed behind all alone. It was only nine o'clock and, as I was not feeling sleepy, I went into the sitting room to watch a film on video. I took my pillow and blanket and, with milk and biscuits, settled down to watch the film.

Halfway through the film I heard a noise just outside the house. I thought it was my imagination so did not bother to go and see what it was. Ten minutes later I heard a noise again, this time coming from my parents' bedroom. I moved quietly to the door and looked through the keyhole.

What I saw frightened me. There were two masked men rummaging through the drawers and cupboards. They were definitely looking for something. I was very frightened and just froze up. My mind stopped working. I did not know what to do. I must have made a noise for the next moment the door opened and one of the men got hold of me. It must have been my reaction to his hold for I kicked him very hard and ran away and hid in my older brother's bedroom. The man kept on calling me telling me that they would not hurt me if I came out. If I didn't they would find me and kill me. At once I recognised the voice which kept on calling me by my name. I knew he would definitely kill me and make it look like an accident. I heard him going through all the rooms. I was glad our house was a bungalow and all the windows were on the ground floor. I quietly opened my brother's bedroom window and slipped out, went to the nearest phone box and called the police.

As I did not want them to escape I quietly went back in and sat on my brother's bed. One of the masked men suddenly came into the room to check again and found me there on the bed. He took me to my parents' bedroom and tied me up. Then he told me that if I ever uttered a word to anyone about them he would definitely come and kill me. That really frightened me and I promised I would not say anything to anyone.

Then suddenly the bedroom door opened with a big bang and there were police all over the place. The men tried to escape but were quickly caught and taken away to the police station. Two policewomen stayed with me until my parents came home. At first they were shocked when they heard what had happened. I was told off by them for being so stupid as to come back into the house but they were very relieved that nothing had happened to me.

From the police my dad found out that his partner was trying to steal the money which my dad had withdrawn from the bank that day to pay his employees the next day. There were twenty-five thousand pounds in all. His friend knew my parents were going to be out until late. What they hadn't bargained on was me being there. I hope I never have to go through that again. It was very frightening and I still cannot believe that I did what I did.

Betrayal

Judgements made sometimes are either for your own good or can bring disaster, like heartbreak. Such a thing happened to me.

I had barely moved into my new home when one sunny day someone knocked on my front door. I opened the door to find a good-looking young man, who happened to be a plumber. He had come to check the plumbing system in my kitchen. He had blond hair, blue eyes and a good physique. His name was Brian.

I felt an instant attraction which was returned by him as well but both being too shy to make the first move we kept quiet. He would come almost every week to have either tea or coffee. I would look forward to his visits. We would sit and talk for ages about anything and everything, except our feelings.

This went on for six months. One day, I was feeling very low. A friend of mine had borrowed some money and was very reluctant to give it back. I had a very big argument with him which made me very sad because when he needed the money, I had been there to lend it to him but now that I needed it, he did not have any. After he went, Brian came for his usual cup of tea and chat. Seeing me upset, he asked me what was wrong. I told him. He just sat there and listened. He asked me if I wanted him to talk to this person. Brian was very understanding and stayed with me for two hours just talking.

When he was leaving, just on the spur of the moment, he kissed me on the cheek. From that moment my feelings became deeper for him but still I was too shy to say anything.

A week later on, Brian asked me out for a drink. I accepted his invitation to go out the next day. He said he would come to collect me at nine o'clock.

The following day was a Saturday, so I did not have to go to work. I took my time getting ready so that he would appreciate my company. Exactly at nine o'clock Brian came to collect me, but changed his mind and said that he would rather stay at home if I didn't mind. He had brought a few beer cans for himself and two bottles of wine for me. I did not mind at all as I also, discreetly, wanted to be alone with him. It looked like he must have read my mind!

So we decided to stay in. He opened his can of beer and I got two wine glasses and a few snacks to go with the drinks and had my first glass of wine with him after not drinking for more than two years.

One glass led to another and soon the bottle was finished. Brian had his cans of beer then started drinking the wine. All the time while we were drinking, all we talked about was my work, this country and his country, as he comes from Ireland. The time passed so quickly that we did not even realise that our drinks were finished too. It was already two o'clock in the morning and Brian decided that after he had helped me clean up, he would go home. For some reason unknown to me, I did not want him to leave and said so. He said that he too did not want to leave.

Then he held me and kissed me. I felt like I was in seventh heaven. I did not want this moment to end but too soon it was already five o'clock in the morning and I had to let him go. I did not ask him why he had to go because I was too happy myself to think of anything else.

The weekend found me in a dreamland. I did not even

mind him not phoning me on Sunday because I knew I would be seeing him on Monday. The eight weeks that followed were just perfect. I couldn't have been happier.

Then all of a sudden he stopped coming to see me or even phoning me. Whenever I phoned him, he never answered. It was always his friend who picked up the phone and said that Brian was not in.

Then one day I phoned once more, and his friend confessed to me that Brian was married and I was just a challenge to him as I did not jump in bed with him the first day he came to my house for tea.

What a fool I was to think that I had something special going with someone as good looking as Brian. Since then my trust in men has gone and from now on I will never make a fool of myself again, ever.

An Ace, the Winning Card

I hated the day when spades were drawn on me and an 'A' printed on my opposite corners. I did not mind being an ace, but I wanted hearts drawn on me instead of spades. I was very envious of the ace which had hearts because it looked so beautiful, unlike me, all black and white and dull. I was packed in a box with another fifty-one cards plus two extra with 'Joker' written on them.

My destination was a place called Victoria Casino. My pack was kept intact in the casino's storeroom. As time went by I thought I was forgotten and would just lie there unseen, unopened and unused. I started feeling very miserable and thought that because I wished to be an ace of hearts, God was taking his revenge on me for not being happy with what I was and wishing for more.

Almost a year had gone by and I was resigned to the fact that I was not wanted anywhere or by anybody, when the storeman picked up my pack among a few others and took us upstairs. My pack was put on the blackjack table where it was opened by the dealer. He shuffled us and put us in a plastic container from which only one card at a time could be drawn upside down then and placed the right way up in the front of the gamblers and the dealer too.

I was played quite a few times either on the dealer's side or the gambler's side. Sometimes I made them win and sometimes they lost.

It was nearing the end of the evening when I really

became lucky for an old couple. The stakes on our table were one hundred pounds at a time. This couple had sat down with five thousand pounds. Poor people, they had been unlucky right from the beginning and they had only two hundred pounds left. They took one last chance and placed all the money on the next card which was to be drawn. They already had the nine of diamonds. If the gentleman before this couple had asked for the next card they would have lost their last ever bet, but he refused as he already had a total of eighteen. The couple kept their fingers crossed and I was drawn and placed in front of them. There are no words that could describe their joy at seeing me but the worst wasn't over yet because the dealer had a total of twelve and the next card or two might still have changed everything because if the dealer drew nine, the couple would have lost their money. It looks like I was meant to change their luck and the dealer drew first four and then seven, so he was bust.

Can you imagine the joy of the couple when they doubled their money? After that until closing time they kept on winning and went home with nine thousand pounds.

I felt so proud of myself and for the couple as well.

When the casino closed for business that day the couple asked the dealer if they could buy my pack from him. The dealer too was very happy with the couple's windfall and gave my pack to them. When the couple returned home the wife took me out of my pack and put me in her handbag. Next day, she bought a small frame and framed me and also gave me a title, 'The Winning Card' and gave the frame to her husband as a memento.

From that moment on, I have taken pride of place on the mantelpiece. I am glad that I have brought joy to this lovely couple. They were foolish enough to take that much money to gamble in the first place but as they never had a holiday in their entire life and they wanted to see the world just once, they had thought they might double their savings and have the holiday which they always craved for. But now with their dreams fulfilled I don't think they will ever make the mistake of gambling their savings again.

One Day in the Life of a One Pound Coin

I have been on so many journeys in my life that I have lost count, sometimes handed from one to the other or just kept in someone's piggy-bank for a long time until needed.

I remember a very unusual day which I will never forget as long as I am around.

On this particular morning I felt very tired and just wanted to be left alone for a little while but my owner had other ideas. He was a fourteen year old boy and on his summer holidays from school. On that day, after a late breakfast, he took me to a gambling machine. He was desperate to have a watch which could be seen through the glass panel so he put me in the slot. I fell down among other coins. Unluckily he lost me and the watch.

In the afternoon the owner of the machine took us out of the little box at the bottom of the machine. He put me and another nineteen coins in a red plastic bag and, with some other bags, took us to the bank. I was handed over the counter to the clerk who counted us again and I was put in the till. Barely an hour had passed when I heard a gunshot and the clerks were told to hand over the money otherwise they would be shot dead. I was handed over the counter to the man with the gun with other coins and notes which he took and put in his bag. In a hurry to get away from the bank he did not realise that the bag had a small hole in it.

He put us on the back seat of the car, climbed in beside us and his friend drove the car away. It was a long drive, but in no time the driver parked the car in his garage and locked the garage doors. While he was taking us out of the car, the bag I was in fell through the hole and split open. The two men were in too much of a hurry to notice that we had fallen out in the car.

Twenty minutes later the driver took the car back to the rental place as he had rented it for the day. The attendant took the car for a wash before renting it out again. While he was cleaning inside the car he found me with the other coins. Instead of telling the owner, he pocketed us. Later on he went to a chip shop for some chips and handed me over the counter. There I was put in the till until, in the early evening, the shop owner's son came to take over. As the owner was leaving he took me with some other coins out of the till so that he could go down to the local pub down the road. He bought a pint and handed me over to the barman who put me in their till. There I stayed until eleven o'clock in the evening at which point I was once again, just by coincidence, handed over to the chip shop owner with his change when he bought yet another pint of beer with a five pound note. He took me back to the chip shop so that he could help his son close up the shop for the day. There once again I was put in the till among the other coins. There I stayed until the next day, when once again my roller-coaster life started again. That was one most unusual day which I will never forget as long as I live.

Adventures of a Carrot

My first recollection of myself was lying in a big compound among other carrots. We were then sprayed with water and cleansed of any mud that was stuck on us.

I was then put into a small box and put on a truck to be taken to a fruit and vegetable market. On the way there, as the roads were very uneven, I was thrown out of the box on to the side of the road. I lay there on the side of the road for a whole day without anyone noticing me.

The next day I was feeling very lonely and rejected when an old lady passing by saw me, picked me up and took me home. There she washed me and put me into the fridge with some more carrots and other vegetables. Everyday she would add one vegetable or another to us.

One day, she took us all out and put us in different piles. She was just deciding which of us to cook when her next-door neighbour came and asked if the old lady had any carrots that she could spare. Apparently the old lady's neighbours always came to her to ask for something or other which they could have as they knew that the old lady liked picking up anything edible and always helped them.

So I with some other carrots was given to this neighbour who took us to her house. From there, her daughter took me to her school the next day. After her lunch she took me to a big kitchen. It was her home economics lesson. There she grated me and put me into a mixing bowl with other ingredients together with flour and eggs. Then she took a wooden spoon and started stirring us all together until I became a thick paste. She then put me into a greased tin and put the tin into a preheated oven to be cooked for thirty minutes. I was then taken out of the tin and placed on a cooling tray.

After I had cooled down I was then placed into a plastic container and taken back to her house.

In the evening I was cut into two pieces, one to be eaten by the family and her mother took the other to the old lady from whom she had borrowed me. So in the end, I ended up in two places at the same time.

Prem Nivas, the House of Love

On one glorious morning my foundations were laid by a five year old boy.

His name was Amit and he had very rich parents. He was the apple of their eyes since he was the only son and because they had been trying for a child for the past twenty years and their wish had finally been granted. When Amit was four years old his parents decided to build a house on a beautiful hillside where the back would have the view of the slope and the front of the house would have the most glorious view of the little valley below with the scenery of lovely colours and smell of the flowers in summer and evergreen trees, and full of snow in winter.

Me, I just want to be the envy of everybody, when the builders are through with me.

Once the foundations were laid the contractor and the builders started building the outside walls. Plumbing was done for downstairs. Then I had concrete poured on my foundations and the ground within the walls. Builders started putting up scaffolding and then seven feet off the ground floor, I had my first layer of beams fitted in vertically after which two more layers were fitted horizontally and vertically again. This pattern went on twice more with a gap of ten feet on each level. On the last layer of the beams I had my roof built again with wooden beams. Then more plumbing was done. I was beginning to take shape now. I hated it with no proper roof or walls because when it rained I became soaking wet or in the heat of the summer so hot that I wished I had a fan around me to keep me cool. Dogs and stray animals would come and pee on me. I just could not wait to be completed.

Builders started building my walls and then partitions were done to give me rooms. I had a kitchen, bathroom, dining room, laundry room and a large sitting room downstairs. Stairs were built to go to a cellar which was seven feet high. I had shelves built in there so that food and vegetables and also drinks could be stored there for freshness and coolness. A spiral staircase was built from one corner of the dining room to go upstairs which has five rooms and yet another big bathroom. Four rooms would become bedrooms but the fifth room was to become a lovely temple, their own worshipping place. Amit's mother was a great believer in God. Even when the doctors said that she couldn't have any children, she never gave up hope and became a true believer when her hopes became a reality. In the attic above the bedrooms pull-up stairs were attached from the hallway.

Next I had electricity put into me. Now I was beginning to look like a house. Once the builders had finished with me, decorators took over. All my rooms were decorated in beautiful colours of green, pastel, light blue and some places just pure white. The kitchen and bathrooms were tiled from floor to ceiling. I had ceiling lights fitted in the sitting room and dining room which were concealed by white plastic tiles.

Once I was completed the owners had a garage and driveway built outside the house and adjoining the laundry room. Gardeners were hired to do the landscaping and plant different but exotic and beautiful flowering shrubs and plants. A greenhouse was built on the far side of the garden for herbs and vegetables which need constant warmth although a vegetable patch was also prepared on the side of the greenhouse. A special playground was also built for Amit.

When I was completed the owners moved into me and made me into a loving home. All I now feel is their love and warmth, and Amit's bubbly laughter all around me. They also named me by calling me Prem Nivas. I hope I bring them joy, happiness and prosperity in all the years to come.

A Statue

What a miserable life I led. All I had been doing for two years was sitting in one corner doing nothing but gathering dust. I was a twelve stone brass statue of a lion. Once I was the pride and joy of someone's front entrance but then I was sold off to the scrapyard like an unwanted piece of furniture.

But then all that changed as out of the blue one day I was bought by a middle-aged man. He took me to his small workplace. The place was empty except for a hot furnace in the middle of the room and a few tools, a slab which looked like a table in one corner of the room and two workers who worked for this man.

It took two men to lift me from the car into the work-place. Here I found out that this man had created quite a few masterpieces in brass statues and was a very well-known person. To him anything he did was a challenge. He created something new every time and the public loved his work.

Next day, I was cleaned properly before being lowered into the melting pot and placed on the top of the furnace. I started to melt after an hour and soon became a thick bubbling liquid. Two-thirds of me was then poured into one mould and the rest of me was poured into another smaller mould. I was left there for the rest of the day. To me all this followed a familiar pattern as before when I was made into a lion. The only thing was, at this time I did not know that my final outcome would be.

Next day, when I was set enough to be moulded into a figurine, part of me was taken out of the smaller mould and the man who bought me set about to work on me. As I was still soft enough to be moulded yet again he made me into a slab with a tiger's face created on the front.

Then my creator took the other part of me out of the bigger mould and set about working on me. This time he created a man in a sitting position with a snake round his neck, beaded necklaces down to his waist, both his hands resting in his lap, and last at the top of his head he created a bun in which there was yet another face from which a shower of water flowed down. On the right side of the man he made a spear with three points, which later I found was called a trisul.

It took the sculptor two weeks to create me into something completely different. I was no longer a lion but a statue called Shiva.

Once I was completed, I was sold to a gentleman who shipped me to London to his brother's house. There I was put into the temple in his house which he had built specially for his family. This family believed fervently in Lord Shiva.

Just imagine my pride and joy at knowing what I have become. To me I am still me but to these people I represent a symbol of Lord Shiva. They light a candle in front of me every morning and pray to me. I am so glad that at last I will not be left in some storeroom to gather dust and I hope to bring them all the luck, love and joy in the future.

The Spirit of Christina

1997

During these last few years in the convent, away from all
the hustle and bustle of city life, Sophie had at last found
peace and penance for the guilt that she carried in her heart
since being here.

Her life had been a turmoil of events ever since she was
thirteen years old. Only since she has been in the convent
has Sophie managed to control her temper and instantane-
ous actions. Any of her friends or her parents who saw her
now would believe she was the Sophie they had come to
know. She did not have many friends, and what friends she
had started getting further and further away from her. In
the end only one had remained, her childhood friend, Ella.

1970–1986

Christina was born into a wealthy family. Both her parents
were busy running their chain of clothes stores all over
Britain from their main office in London. Sometimes they
had to go to other stores to see how they were running and
also that there were no problems or hiccups so they
travelled a lot.

Christina was only three months old when her mother
decided to start work again and as her parents were very
much in love they did not like to stay apart from each other

for long, if possible. Even though they both loved Christina, sometimes they thought that she was an unwanted third so as soon as she was born a full-time nanny was hired to look after Christina.

As Christina grew up she started becoming very rebellious and spoilt. She would get up to mischief just to get her parents' attention. She loved her parents very much but they never had time for her. To get Christina off their hands as quickly as possible her parents would oblige her every little whim. The more Christina craved for her parents' loving attention, the more she got into trouble. In the end her parents, having no patience for Christina, sent her to a boarding school when she was only six years old. Instead of getting better she became worse. She would bully the other kids, take their toys and would sometimes beat them up.

Her parents became very frustrated with her behaviour. Within the span of five years, Christina had been expelled from many boarding schools. In the end her parents had to bring her back home. They hired a tutor for Christina who would come every day to teach her at home.

Christina wondered why her parents could not understand that all she needed was their love. She craved for the kind of love that her nanny gave her, but Nanny was not her mother or father. All they could think about was themselves and making more money. To Christina money was nothing if there was no love involved.

In the end she gave up trying to get their attention all the time and did her own thing.

On her sixteenth birthday Christina asked her parents for a sports car. 'You don't know how to drive, Christina. You will get a car when you can drive,' her father said. 'How about a gold bracelet instead?'

'I don't want a bracelet, Father. How little you know about me. You don't even know that I learnt to drive when

I was fourteen. My friends taught me how to drive. Now, can I have the car or not?' Christina said angrily. 'I have promised my friends a party at the Hilton Hotel. I want to show off my new car to them.'

'I am sorry, Christina, but you cannot have a car until you have a licence which you will not get until you are seventeen. You will have to wait until next year for your car,' her father replied impatiently. 'Why don't you go with the driver to a jewellery shop and choose whatever you like from there?'

'I don't want any jewellery. I want a car.' Saying this, Christina ran out of the dining room leaving her breakfast untouched.

'How dare he deny me a car. As if he cares what I do or want. I see them twice a year at the breakfast table with me. I don't want any jewellery. Every year for the last five years he has given me jewellery. I don't even wear it because it is not given to me with love. To them it is just an obligation they have to fulfil. And how dare Mother stay quiet. She takes Father's side all the time. Never once has she tried to understand me,' cried Christina as she flung herself on her bed.

Nanny just sat on the bed and listened to her. She had tried talking to Christina's parents when Christina was very young.

'We have hired you to look after Christina, not to tell us what we are lacking. We are doing our best to provide her with a comfortable lifestyle. She has everything she needs. It is up to you to control her,' she had been told.

Since then Nanny never said anything to them but did her best to give Christina the love she craved, but even that was not enough when the girl cried out for her parents' love.

Now she just sat there and let Christina vent her anger through tears. She felt sorry for this girl, but there was nothing she could do except be there for her.

By evening Christina had made up her mind that if her parents did not buy her a car then she would just have to take her mother's sports car. As she was getting ready for the party, there was a knock on her bedroom door. Nanny opened the door to let in her mother.

'Christina, I have come to collect you to take you to the party. Your father and I have a business appointment so we will drop you off at the Hilton. Just phone home when you are ready to leave and the driver will collect you,' Christina's mother said as she entered her daughter's bedroom.

'That is very nice of you, Mother, but I wouldn't want to impose on you or Father to take me to the party. My friends are coming here to get me, so I will go with them,' replied Christina sarcastically.

'As you wish. Enjoy your party, Christina.' Saying this she bade Nanny goodnight and left, leaving the smell of her perfume in her wake.

Christina just stayed quiet. This was not like Christina. Usually she would shout and scream at her mother but not today. I'm sure she is up to something, thought Nanny, but she too did not say anything. She did not want to lecture Christina today of all days. The child was unhappy as it was. She bade Christina goodnight, told her not to be late back from the party and left to go to her own room.

Christina waited half an hour before going downstairs. Her parents had already left. On the hallstand she found her mother's car keys. Taking them, Christina left the house, went to the garage and took out her mother's car. Her friends were waiting at the Hilton for her. As soon as she entered they wanted to know what car she had received for her birthday. Christina did not want her friends to know that she did not get a car for her birthday so she told them that her parents bought her a sports car which was parked at that moment in the hotel car park. She promised them a ride in the car after the party. The party went well.

It was well after midnight when Christina dropped off the last of her friends in her sports car. She did not want to go home yet, so she decided to go for a drive on the M1 motorway. At this time of night the roads would be quiet and she would just enjoy the drive. She had had quite a bit to drink and once on the M1, Christina turned the music up very loud and put her foot down on the accelerator. It felt so good to drive like this. Soon she was in a world of her own. She started to think about her life and where it was leading to.

So deep in thought was she that Christina did not realise that she was really driving very fast. From somewhere in her thoughts she heard the sirens. They were getting louder and louder. She focused her attention on the roads, then looked through her rear-view mirror and realised that they were indeed police sirens and that at least three police cars were following her. They were flashing their lights at her for her to stop her car. Christina became very frightened. Firstly, she did not have a licence and secondly, a quick glance at her speedometer showed she was driving very fast. In her fright, instead of stopping the car Christina tried to get away from the pursuing police cars. In her fright and nervousness, Christina lost control of the car and swerved into the central reservation. The next thing she knew she was trapped in the car as it somersaulted twice and came to a stop in the middle of the road on its roof.

★

Christina came to and found herself standing in front of heaven's gates. They opened on her first knock. She tried to walk through them but something prevented her from entering the gates. Then out of nowhere came a voice:

'Christina, your time on earth has not yet come to an

end. In your life you have not done one single good deed. You have caused your parents unhappiness. They did love you in their own way but because they loved each other very much they did not know how to share their love with you. You will have to go back and repent for what you have done. You will have to do a good deed before you will be let in through these gates.'

'How did I get here? I remember driving my mum's car, the police chase and then the accident. After that I don't remember anything,' Christina asked the voice.

'You were trapped in your car when it burst into flames and you were burnt alive. Do you want to see what you look like now?'

'Yes.'

★

Through the gates Christina saw that she was in an intensive care unit in the hospital. Her body was now covered by a white sheet. She heard running feet and soon the doors burst open as her parents came through them. They came to stand by the bed. At a nod from the doctor, the nurse lifted the cover. One look and her mother turned her face into father's chest. Her father just looked at the burnt body that was supposed to be their daughter. There was nothing left of their beautiful Christina. He wished they had paid more attention to Christina. He couldn't stop his wife crying or banish her anguished look as she just crumpled against him. It seemed as if these last few minutes he too had aged considerably as he wondered what good all his money was now when there was no child left to share it with. He wished he could turn the clock back and show Christina that they really did love her. He wished with all his heart that they had listened to Nanny when she had come to talk to them instead of telling her off.

1973–1986

Sophie grew up in a small town called Cumbernauld in Scotland. She had an older brother called Jack. They were a very close-knit family. Sophie couldn't have asked for better parents. Her parents and Jack doted on her.

Coming from a loving family, Sophie could never bear to see anyone unhappy. She would try her best to make them happy. Her parents were always amazed at her ability to comfort anyone, be it a human being or a stray animal. She grew up to be very beautiful and intelligent. She would never get angry at anyone unless it was necessary and even then she would tell them off mildly.

One day, just before her thirteenth birthday, Sophie and her friends went to the sports centre. There they passed part of the morning playing tennis and badminton. As it was a hot day they all decided to have a swim in the swimming pool. Everyone was enjoying themselves. After playing with her friends in the pool, Sophie decided to swim the length of the pool. Suddenly Sophie felt a cramp in her legs. She did not take any heed and swam on. Soon the cramp became very severe and she felt herself going under the water. Her friends thought that Sophie was swimming under the water as she usually did and did not bother with her much. But after a few minutes when she did not surface, her friends got worried and told the lifeguard. He dived into the water and soon came up with Sophie unconscious in his arms. An ambulance was called and until it arrived the lifeguard and his partner from the other pool tried to revive Sophie. By now her friends had gathered around Sophie and were looking very worried. Soon the ambulance came and took Sophie's lifeless body to the hospital. They tried to revive her. When they reached the hospital they could barely feel her pulse. Sophie's friends had already alerted her parents and Jack who went to the hospital as soon as possible.

1986–1994

'I cannot go back now. Have you seen my body? It's all burnt. What kind of a life am I going to have?' asked Christina, still looking through heaven's gates at the scene in the hospital ICU.

'Well, there is someone else whose body you can possess. Her heart has just stopped but her brain is still functioning. The doctors are trying to get her heart beating again. Now if you hurry, you can go back to earth, keep yourself as well as this girl alive and do what I told you to do,' said the voice gently.

'I am willing to do anything. I don't want to go to hell.'

'There is something I must tell you. When you enter Sophie's body – the girl's name is Sophie – you will forget our conversation. You will forget your previous life. Because in your heart you are bitter about your previous life you will be bringing out the bitterness in Sophie too. Her personality is going to change. Her mind will think logically but her heart will overrule it. Now in all this you will have to keep your promise. Only through your penance will you be free to enter these gates. Are you prepared to do that?'

'If I forget everything, how will I repent?'

'When the time is right, your heart will tell you. Now go, Christina, before it is too late.'

★

Christina felt herself flying down. She entered the emergency room in the hospital. There she saw the doctors around the bed on which Sophie lay helplessly. Christina entered her body.

The doctors trying to get Sophie's heart beating again gave up at last and pronounced her dead. They were talking about asking her parents for Sophie's organs to be donated to help other people when suddenly a bleep came on the monitor which was still attached to the heart. The bleep became louder and stronger. The doctors were baffled. They were certain Sophie had died. It was a miracle to see the life returning. The girl was alive.

Sophie opened her eyes to see a sea of faces looking down on her. She tried to get up but she was told to lie still. The last thing she remembered was swimming then getting the cramp in her legs and water all around her as she was pulled down, and then only blackness as she lost consciousness.

'Where am I? How did I get here?' she asked.

'You are in the hospital, Sophie, and very lucky to be alive. We had all but given up on you. You are one lucky young lady,' said one of the doctors. Looking around properly, Sophie realised that she was indeed in a hospital room and the sea of faces were of three doctors and two nurses.

Sophie stayed in the hospital for a few days. The doctor wanted to make sure that there were no after-effects of her near-death experience. Her parents were told what had happened in the emergency room. Her mother had stayed with her during the first night, too frightened to leave her lovely daughter alone. Jack had brought with him a large bunch of flowers and her favourite teddy bear on the first day. Her friends had also come to see her at the hospital and had brought her little gifts, flowers and chocolates. Sophie herself was so glad to be alive.

★

Sophie had never lost her temper before – she couldn't understand why she did it, but at the time she just couldn't control it.

It happened out of the hospital. They were all in their living room, sitting down to their usual night-cap of a hot chocolate drink each. Sophie saw that her parents were deeply involved in a discussion with Jack concerning his A-level studies. She did not like the way they were ignoring her and only talking to Jack.

'Mum, Dad, I want to talk to you,' said Sophie, trying to break up the conversation they were having with Jack. Suddenly she felt very jealous of Jack and the jealousy tore through her.

'Just a minute, darling,' replied her Dad patiently.

'Now, Dad,' shouted Sophie, causing everyone to look at her in alarm. 'How dare you ignore me and pretend that I am not in the room with you. Jack is everything to you. I am not. You love him more than you love me.'

'What's wrong, Sophie? What brought all this on? You know we all love you,' said her mother as she came to sit beside Sophie.

'No you don't. You would have been glad if I had died.' Saying this, she threw her mug of hot chocolate on the floor and ran out of the room.

They were all stunned into silence by Sophie's actions. She had never before lost her temper like that. She was always considerate and kind to others, so they did not know what had brought this on. Jack told his parents he would go and see Sophie. She always listened to him.

'Sophie, can I come in?' asked Jack as he knocked on her bedroom door.

'Go away, Jack. I don't want to see anyone.'

'Please Sophie, let me in. I only want to help.'

Jack heard the key turn in the lock and he opened the door slowly to see Sophie standing just inside the door with tears streaming down her face. He opened his arms and Sophie just ran into them and cried. Jack just let her cry. When he felt her a little calmer he asked, 'What's wrong, love?'

'I don't know, Jack. One minute I was fine and the next I was angry for no reason at all. I know you all love me. I don't know why I did what I did just now. I'm so sorry, Jack,' replied Sophie with her face buried in her brother's chest.

'You know we all love you. We'll never do anything to hurt you.'

'I know. I'm so sorry.'

'I know. Just go to sleep,' Jack said as he helped her get into her bed and pulled the covers over her. Kissing her forehead he bade her goodnight.

'Jack?'

'Yes, Sophie?' asked Jack from the doorway as he was just about to switch off the lights and close the door.

'Tell Mum and Dad I really am sorry.'

'Yes, Sophie.'

Ever since that night Sophie's personality seemed to have changed. She became aggressive and violent. She would start an argument about little things and cause scenes of unpleasantness no matter where she was. It could either be at home, in school or anywhere. She would always say she was sorry afterwards but the damage would be done already. Her parents dreaded the time when the arguments would start with violent consequences. Even Jack started losing his patience with Sophie. He just could not handle her anymore. When she was nice she was very nice and when nasty she was very nasty. Her parents had consulted many doctors about her behaviour only to be told that sometimes after a near-death experience a person's personality does change. Sophie went to see a specialist in this area. After many years of consultation, Sophie did manage to control her temper but by then it was too late. She had lost all her friends except one, Ella, who stood by her all through this time. Even her parents had no patience for her anymore, not since she had taken her father's car last year without his permission to celebrate her eighteenth birthday alone in Edinburgh some thirty miles away from her home town. She had no friends left now. Even Ella, when she found out what Sophie intended to do, tried to talk her out of it but Sophie would not listen and went alone instead. Coming back at night, and because it was raining heavily, the car skidded and crashed into the back of another car. The car was a write-off. Only Sophie emerged from the accident unhurt. When asked why she did it by her father, she replied, 'As if you care what I do.'

The last straw was when, during Jack's engagement party, for no reason at all Sophie lost her temper with Janice, Jack's fiancée. She had been drinking since early evening. As the evening wore on so Sophie's mood change increased. Her parents dreaded yet another argument on this special day so they urged Jack to talk to Sophie and make her drink some coffee or eat something.

'Sophie, why don't we go into the dining room and eat something? I'm hungry,' asked Jack as he came to stand beside her.

'Why, has Janice deserted you already?' Sophie said sarcastically. 'Just go back to where you belong and leave me alone, Jack. I am all right.'

'If you say. You know where I am if you need me.' Saying this, Jack went back to Janice and started chatting to her. Soon they were both laughing which made Sophie very angry. She went to where Janice and Jack were and started hitting her with her bare hands.

'How dare you laugh at me,' she cried and while still hitting her she asked how she, Janice, dared take her family away from her. She said that even Jack had changed since meeting her.

Jack tried to get Sophie off Janice but she started hitting him too. Suddenly she realised what she was doing, looked around her and saw the stunned onlookers and just ran out of the room.

Her father had had enough of Sophie's tantrums. He went after her to her room and went in without knocking and said, 'That's it, young lady. You either abide by my rules in this house or leave. All of us have taken as much as we can from you. No more, do you hear me? No more!' and he banged the door shut as he went downstairs.

Sophie just stayed face down on her bed. What was happening to her? Why was she making everybody's lives a misery? Her actions today were uncalled for. The sooner she got out of this place the sooner peace and tranquillity would return.

Within a week she had found a job and a rented flat at a reasonable price in Edinburgh. She told her parents she would be moving out the next day.

'It's no use me saying sorry every time I do something wrong. I still keep on hurting you. The best thing to do is leave you all and try to find myself again.'

They did not know what to say. In a way they were pleased that Sophie was doing something positive but on the other hand they were sad to see her move out. Not only was she moving but she was moving to a different town altogether.

That day Sophie went to see her friend Ella, and told her her news.

'I will miss you, Sophie. You have always told me everything you feel and do. We have always stayed friends, no matter what. I will stand by you, my friend. Just keep in touch with me. I promise I will come and visit you. You too must come and visit me,' Ella told her friend.

They spent the day together talking about everything

and nothing in particular, and promised to keep in touch with each other. Ella was sad to see her friend leave in the evening. She had known Sophie since they were both toddlers, and they had grown up in each other's company, but since Sophie's drowning experience, she had changed completely. Even that did not stop Ella being her friend and she stood by her side. She prayed that maybe Sophie might find the change of environment and being away from here soothing for her and her temper.

Sophie left the next day, to start her life alone in Edinburgh, promising to write to her parents and phone them as soon as she was settled. She felt as if her family were relieved to see her go and it broke her heart, but she couldn't blame them for feeling that way. She had made up her mind that she would try and change for them. She just could not understand why she behaved like this and then as soon as her temper had cooled she would feel sorry, promising herself she would not do it again. Then something would happen and she would snap, and do something drastic, unable to stop herself from doing it.

Sophie enjoyed her work as a receptionist very much. This last year had been soul-searching for her. It was very hard for her to make new friends. She was frightened in case she made a scene here too. Her colleagues at work thought she was stuck-up, that they were no good for her, so they left her alone.

Sophie did not stay far from where she worked so she walked to and from work. As it was Friday she went into the local supermarket to buy some groceries. Ella was coming over tonight and would be staying until Sunday night. Sophie was looking forward to seeing her friend again. After leaving Cumbernauld, Sophie never went back again. Her parents and Jack would come up to see her whenever they had a chance. Sophie and Janice had made up but all of them were still treading carefully around each other. The only person who was free and more friendly was Ella.

So deep in thought was she that Sophie practically bumped into someone in front of her and sent them both tumbling down on to the floor. The next thing she realised was that she was lying on top of a gorgeous man looking into his beautiful brown eyes.

'Hi, beautiful, I'm Andrew. Who are you? No one has ever introduced themselves to me like this before. I'm honoured,' said Andrew, still lying on the floor with Sophie atop him. Their groceries had gone flying across the floor and his arms had come around her. Sophie tried to get up but she was trapped against this man with his arms around her. Slowly he let her go and helped her stand up.

'I'm sorry, I was not looking where I was going,' replied Sophie softly. She was still trembling after the encounter with this gorgeous man. She had never experienced a feeling like this before. The shopkeeper had come to help them with their groceries and was giving them both sly looks. By the look of things, the shopkeeper thought, it won't be long before these two young ones started seeing each other.

'Hi, I'm Andrew,' said Andrew again and extended his hand. 'It's nice to meet you.'

'Sorry, I'm Sophie,' replied Sophie shyly as she extended her hand which was immediately taken into a strong grip. 'I'm really sorry about this.'

'How about coming out for a drink with me, Sophie?' Andrew asked this beautiful lady with beautiful almond shaped blue eyes and dark long hair that nearly reached her waist.

'We hardly know each other.'

'Well we can get to know each other over a drink and meal if you like.'

'Sorry, but I'm busy this weekend.'

'Got a boyfriend? If you have then just say so and I will not bother you any further although I would really like to get to know you better.'

Sophie was pleased by Andrew's frankness. She too liked him and would like to get to know him better.

'Nothing like that,' she replied. 'I have a girlfriend who is coming over to stay with me for the weekend. Maybe next time.'

'I look forward to seeing you again soon. How about meeting me on Monday evening?' asked Andrew.

They agreed to meet on Monday evening as they both left after finishing off their shopping. That evening Sophie told Ella about her encounter with Andrew and how she thought she was already falling in love with him. Ella was pleased for her friend. She hoped that at last Sophie would settle down. She remembered when one by one all of Sophie's friends had deserted her. It was not Sophie's fault that she had undergone a personality change after that dreadful swimming accident.

Sophie couldn't wait to see Andrew again. She had promised Ella that she would phone her the next evening and tell her how her date with Andrew went.

They had been going out with each other for three months when they decided to get engaged and to marry a couple of months after that. Sophie found out that she and Andrew had a lot in common. Andrew's parents had died in a plane crash six years ago when Andrew was twenty. He had no brothers and sisters, or any living relatives. As he was the sole heir, he had inherited his father's business. He was a shrewd businessman and in the last six years since taking over his father's business, it had flourished tremendously.

Sophie phoned her parents and told them about the engagement and said that she would bring Andrew over the next weekend to meet them. They were very pleased and told her that they were looking forward to meeting Andrew.

Her parents liked Andrew very much. They had arranged a surprise party for them both. For once the party went well and without a single hitch. Sophie's parents thought that at last Sophie had calmed down and that it would do her good to settle down. They talked about the wedding and that evening the date was set for a spring wedding in April which was only two months away.

For the first time in a long time Sophie saw that her parents and Jack were very happy and content. She too was happy now that she had Andrew. They all promised to see each other soon and go over the wedding plans.

A week before the wedding Sophie went home alone. She was to get married in her home town church. All the arrangements had been made by her parents and Jack. He too had set the date for his wedding that summer. All Sophie had to do was to have last minute alterations made to her mother's wedding gown. Her mother wanted Sophie to wear that. Everything was going well.

Andrew arrived two days before the wedding on a Thursday. He came over to the house that evening with his friend Simon who was to be his best man. They had booked into a hotel until Saturday when after the wedding both Sophie and Andrew would be flying off to the Bahamas for their honeymoon.

Everyone had gathered at the house including a few friends of Jack, Janice and Ella. Everything was going well. Drinks were flowing and all were enjoying themselves.

Sophie looked around for Andrew and saw him talking to a friend of Janice's. From where she was it looked like they were having a good time. Jealousy tore through her heart but she kept quiet. As the evening wore on so her jealousy increased. Every time Andrew left her side it seemed he went to this same girl. There came a point when

Sophie could contain her jealousy and anger no more when she saw Andrew leave the room with this girl. She went after them and found Andrew in the kitchen, but the girl was nowhere to be seen.

'Where is she?' she asked with anger emanating from her eyes.

'Who are you talking about?' Andrew asked her in surprise. He had never before seen Sophie this angry.

'The girl you have been chatting to all evening. I saw the way you two were cosily talking to each other. I saw you leaving the room with her. Where is she?' Sophie was by now very angry.

'We did come out of the room together but she has gone home. I just came into the kitchen to have something to eat. You don't have to be jealous, love. I love you. After all, we'll be getting married on Saturday,' Andrew said calmly.

'Don't try to fool me, Andrew. I saw the way you two were talking all evening. Have you sent her to your hotel room so that you can meet her there? Is she more interesting than me?' She screamed at Andrew as he turned away from her in disgust.

'You are drunk, Sophie. Go and lie down and I will talk to you tomorrow,' he said still with his back to her.

This snapped Sophie's patience. Before she knew what she was doing she picked up a knife and shouted his name. As Andrew turned around to face her again Sophie stabbed him very hard with the knife. Then in disbelief she saw him slump to the floor. She looked at her hands which were covered by his blood and the knife still held in her right hand. In disgust and fear she threw the knife away from her, looked around her, then looked at Andrew. He was lying very still.

'God, I have killed him,' she muttered. In fear of getting caught and being sent to prison for Andrew's murder, Sophie ran out of the house from the kitchen door which led out on to the garden. The side gate allowed her to get out. Sophie couldn't remember how long she ran for. At one point she washed her blood-soaked hands in a nearby stream, made herself presentable and then kept on running for her life.

★

Sophie had been on the run for nearly a month. During the daytime she would hide in the fields and mountains and at night she would try to get away as far as possible. She tried to keep off the main roads in case the police were looking for her.

One evening she came to a big church. She thought that no one would be there at this time of the night so she tried the front door but it was locked. Then she tried the back door and luckily it opened at the first attempt. Sophie entered the church, closed the door behind her and went inside. It seemed very large from inside. She passed through some rooms looking for a safe place to sleep when suddenly she came upon the main part of the church. Sophie felt so much at peace here that she went to one of the pews and went to sleep on it. She didn't know how long she could keep this up. She was getting very tired. She would have to find a safe sanctuary to hide in soon. She could not go on like this. With these thoughts in her mind Sophie fell asleep.

Mother Mary found a young girl fast asleep on the church pew and wondered how she got there. By the look of her and her clothes, this girl was very poor and hungry. She was so thin. Very gently Mother Mary woke Sophie up.

As soon as Sophie opened her eyes she sat up quickly. There was a nun standing in front of her.

'I'm sorry. I will go away promptly. I meant to be away before anyone arrived here,' said Sophie in a frightened voice.

When Mother Mary saw how frightened this girl was she said, 'Don't be frightened. I am Mother Mary. How did you get here? Who are you, child?'

'My name is Sophie. Is this a convent? I have been looking for a sanctuary for some time. Can I stay here, please?' asked Sophie pleadingly.

'Yes, this is a convent and you are welcome to stay here as long as you like. Care to tell me why you are looking for sanctuary?'

When Sophie remained quiet, Mother Mary said, 'Don't worry. Tell me when you are ready. I will tell Sister Julie to show you to your room. After you have bathed and rested, come down and I will tell you what your duties will be.'

Mother Mary left to get Sister Julie. While she was gone Sophie looked around her. It was such a nice, tranquil place. After the events and turmoil of the past month Sophie needed this very badly. She did not know what she intended to do about Andrew's murder but she definitely needed time alone very badly. If need be then she would stay here permanently.

Soon she settled down to convent life.

1997

Mother Mary had never asked Sophie why she had stayed on in the convent this long. The girl was very helpful and pulled more than her weight around the place but she knew that Sophie carried a heavy burden of guilt in her heart. Whatever it is, if Sophie wants to tell me then she still will, thought Mother Mary. She had come to love and care for her. Anyway she hoped that Sophie had at last found the peace which she craved so badly.

Sophie had enjoyed the peaceful existence of the convent during the past three years, but she knew now that she would never be at peace completely until she had confessed her crime to the police.

So, with her mind made up, Sophie went to Mother Mary and told her everything. After listening to her, Mother Mary said, 'I'm glad you are going to own up to your crime, Sophie. I have enjoyed having you here, but you must do what you think is right. These doors will always be open to you, dear. Now, be off and God be with you.'

So, with Mother Mary's blessing Sophie left the next day to give herself up at the police station. She took a train from Dundee to Cumbernauld. She hadn't realised that she had travelled that far on foot when she was on the run after killing Andrew.

She went straight to the police station and told them that she had come to give herself up for the murder of Andrew. They asked her what her name was. When she answered them they looked it up in their files for the date on which Sophie said she had committed the murder.

After checking their records the policeman at the desk asked Sophie to wait a second. He disappeared inside. When he came out he had a policewoman with him. She asked Sophie to go with her into a side room where Sophie was once again told to wait until someone could come and take her statement.

Nearly an hour had gone by and still no one had come to take her statement. In this time she was offered tea or a cold drink which Sophie declined. She was very nervous about the outcome of the whole episode. She knew that the sentence for murder would definitely be imprisonment, how long for, she did not know, but she deserved whatever she got.

'Why are they taking so long? Why has no one come to talk to me?' Sophie asked the policewoman when she came in yet again to ask Sophie if she needed anything.

'It won't be long now, Sophie. We are short of staff and there is no one here to take your statement so we had to call someone out from another station. Looks like they are busy too. You are sure you don't need anything?' asked the policewoman.

'No, thank you. I just cannot wait to get this over and done with,' said Sophie nervously.

The policewoman just smiled at Sophie and left the room silently. Suddenly the door burst open and a policeman came in. Sophie stood up and looked at the open doorway with a shocked expression on her face as she looked at the man who had followed in the policeman's wake. Then Sophie felt herself falling as she fainted but before she fell to the ground she was caught in Andrew's strong arms.

★

'Come, Christina, it's time for you to come and join us,' said the voice.

Christina felt herself leave Sophie's body and found herself once again outside heaven's gates. Now she remembered everything, including being in Sophie's body.

'But I haven't repented for my crimes, and instead of doing a good deed I killed Andrew.'

'No, child, you stabbed Andrew all right but you did not wait to see whether he was alive or dead. You ran away instead. But you have paid the price for your actions. Your penance was your sanctuary in the convent where you worked very hard and helped others. Your good deed was coming back to give yourself up to the police. You brought Andrew and Sophie back together. You can now enter the gates of heaven, child,' replied the voice.

But now Christina did not want to enter the gates so she

asked, 'Can I go back on the earth and help people who need my help? I would like to be their guardian angel and help the ones who need my help.'

'So be it, child. You have my blessing.'

'If I need your help and advice, I can come and talk to you, can't I?' asked Christina.

'Of course, child, whenever you want to. Now go and help a lost soul.'

The first thing Christina did was to go and see what had happened to Andrew and Sophie. It seemed as if she had been talking to the voice at heaven's gate for a long time but in actual fact it was only a few minutes.

★

Andrew was still at the police station sitting on a chair with Sophie still held in his arms. Andrew was talking to her softly. The policeman and policewoman had left them alone and asked Andrew to call them if they needed them.

Slowly Sophie came round to the feeling of being held in the comfort of strong arms. She did not want to wake up from the dream that she was having at the moment. It felt so real. Even Andrew's voice sounded real but it couldn't be real. She knew if she opened her eyes the dream would disappear and reality would return. Andrew was dead and that was reality. But his voice kept on urging her to open her eyes. Slowly she opened her eyes to see that she really was in Andrew's arms.

'But you are dead.'

'No darling, as you can see I am not dead. I am alive and well.'

'But how? I saw you dead. I stabbed you and killed you.'

'You did stab me but you did not kill me, darling. It was foolish of you to run away. I have looked everywhere for you, reported you missing all over Britain. Where did you go to?' asked Andrew.

Sophie told him everything. When she finished Andrew said that they were going home to see her parents. This frightened her but Andrew reassured her that they too had been worried about her, and that they had told him everything about Sophie's past. He told Sophie that no matter what he still loved her and wanted to marry her. Sophie just burst out crying and promised never to hurt him again. He kissed her then and soon they left to go to see her parents.

On the way Sophie asked Andrew how he knew that she was at the police station to which he replied that he had told the police that if they found her they were to call him and no one else no matter in which part of the country she was found. When she turned up at the police station they phoned him and told him and he came straight away.

★

It made Christina feel good to see something good come out of all this and so, leaving them, she went on her adventures as a guardian angel.

Rose Princess

Once upon a time, far away in a mountainous country called Montania, there lived a king and queen in a huge castle which was surrounded by a moat.

The view that greeted everyone, the royals and Montania's citizens every day, was beautiful. The castle itself was in the middle of a valley surrounded by four huge mountains. In spring and summer, all you could see was beautiful wild flowers and trees with green leaves. In autumn these leaves changed to golden brown, giving the impression that the mountains were covered in gold when the sun shone on them. And in the winter all the countryside and the mountains were covered in snow. It was like living in paradise because the King made sure that his people were always happy and content.

The King had two sons; Prince Randall and, two years younger than him, Prince Robert. They were complete opposites. While Prince Robert was kind, friendly and generous, Prince Randall was always a handful. He was always rude to the servants, guards and Montania's citizens too. He used to look down on them all. He wanted everyone to do his bidding. If anyone made a mistake they would end up being whipped by him.

The King thought that getting him married might change him so he had Prince Randall married to his friend's daughter, Princess Maria from the neighbouring country but even that did not change him. Even though he was good to his wife, his attitude where the public were concerned was still the same. To him everyone who was not of noble birth was of no importance, and he treated them as such. Prince Robert on the other hand treated everyone as his equal no matter what their caste or religion. He could never understand why his brother behaved in such a monstrous way.

Robert had fallen in love with Princess Maria's sister, Princess Angela, on his brother's wedding day but it took him three years to confess his feelings towards Princess Angela to his sister-in-law. He told Princess Maria about it and asked her to talk to the King. Princess Maria was very happy. She liked Prince Robert very much and knew he would never treat her sister like her husband treated her. Even though Prince Randall was good to her, Princess Maria knew that he did not love her and had been unfaithful to her within a year of their marriage.

The King was pleased with Princess Maria's choice of the bride for his younger son. Recently he had been in a dilemma about relinquishing the throne to one of his sons. He knew by right it should be the oldest son but because of Randall's behaviour towards Montania's citizens he knew that his country would be in ruins in no time. His people had been very happy under his rule but they would be very unhappy under the rule of his eldest son so the King knew in his heart that his younger son would be the one who would take over the throne from him. He knew that Prince Randall would not be happy but that was just too bad. He could not allow his citizens to be unhappy.

Princess Maria was seven months' pregnant when Prince Robert got married to her sister Princess Angela. The whole country celebrated on their wedding day. They liked Prince Robert a lot and prayed that he would have a very long, happy married life. He was always kind to them and always asked after their health. He was nothing like

Prince Randall and they hoped that the King would see fit to crown Prince Robert as their new king instead of Prince Randall.

One evening, soon after the wedding of Prince Robert, Prince Randall was passing his father's chambers on his way out to meet his mistress when he heard voices coming from within the chambers. Being of a nosy disposition as well, Prince Randall stood just outside the door to listen in on the conversation. Only last week he had had a big argument with his father, the King, about how it was time for the King to step down and crown him the next king.

'I will think about it and let you know soon,' the King had said.

'What is there to think about? As it is you are not in good health and I am old enough to take over the running of the country,' Prince Randall had persisted.

'You will know of my decision soon enough,' the King had replied and had left it at that.

Now outside his father's chambers, Prince Randall hoped that he might be able to find out when he would become the next king. He always though his father was too lenient with matters concerning their country. It was about time all this changed. He would show the King and citizens of Montania how to rule the country. If they did not obey him, he would either put them in the dungeons or have them beheaded. Soon they all would be under his command. He could just see his dream becoming a reality. He was jolted out of his dreams when he heard his father reply to something that his mother had said.

'But how can I trust him? He will ruin the whole country. No, I have made up my mind that Robert will be crowned as the new king next week and if Randall does not like it then he can leave the country for ever. I have had enough complaints about him.'

'Very well, whatever you think best. I hope Randall will

stand by his brother and help him run the country,' Prince Randall heard his mother reply.

He did not wait a second more outside the chambers but returned to his quarters.

'I thought you were going out for the evening. What happened?' asked Princess Maria cautiously when she saw her husband enter their quarters with anger and hatred visible in his face and eyes.

Prince Randall hardly heard what his wife said as he uttered in an angry voice, 'Like hell I will let that happen. I will kill him before he becomes king and will also kill my father if he tries to deny me my right to the throne. Who does he think he is? I am the eldest of the two and I should have the throne, not him. Goody Two-shoes, I always knew he would be a threat to me. He will not live to see the sunrise tomorrow.'

Saying that he started walking towards the door. Princess Maria became very frightened when she heard this and knew it was Prince Robert who her husband was talking about. She knew enough about her husband to know that he would carry out his threat. She ran after him to try to stop him from doing something awful which he might regret at a later date. No amount of persuasion would convince Prince Randall. He was in such a dark rage that he did not see anything beyond losing his right to the throne. They were both on top of the stairs when Prince Randall became very angry and lost his temper. In a blind fury he lashed out at his wife who lost her balance and fell down the stairs. Realising what he had done, Prince Randall ran down the stairs shouting at his wife who now lay unconscious at the bottom of the stairs.

Hearing the commotion outside, both the King and Queen came out to see what was happening. Soon they were followed by Prince Robert and Princess Angela. The sight that greeted them all was terrible. Prince Randall was kneeling beside his wife and shouting for help. Soon, between himself and Prince Robert, they had Princess Maria upstairs in their quarters. She looked very pale and was hardly breathing at all. Soon a doctor was called for.

When the doctor arrived he told everyone to wait outside. Ten minutes later he emerged from the quarters looking very dejected. He told them that Princess Maria was dead and so was the child who she was carrying inside her. Up until now Prince Randall had remained quiet, but hearing the doctor's words he suddenly realised how much he loved his wife and how much he would miss not only her but her unborn child as well. He looked at his father and brother with contempt in his eyes and said to his father, 'It's your fault that Maria is dead. I will never forgive any one of you. I wish I hadn't heard you talking to mother tonight. Otherwise she would never have come running after me, and I would not have lost my temper and sent her flying down the stairs.'

Shocked into stunned silence after hearing Prince Randall speak with contempt, the King soon recovered and told him, 'Eavesdroppers never hear anything good about themselves. I am glad that you now know my intentions. After what's happened tonight I am sure that what I intend to do is right. If you wish to stay in the castle you will have to abide by my rules or else leave the country.'

'I would rather leave the country than become second fiddle to someone.' Saying this, Prince Randall looked at his brother with hate-filled eyes before returning his gaze to his father. 'But I will be back. You mark my words.'

With those parting words he left the castle. Prince Robert tried to follow him to talk to him to try to get him to come back but the King forestalled him. 'Let him go, son. He will soon come to his senses and come back. He has had it easy all his life. Let him learn the hard way,' he said.

Princess Maria was buried in the royal cemetery just outside at the back of the castle. Everyone hoped that Prince Randall might at least come for the funeral but he did not show up.

Princess Angela missed her sister very much. They had been very close. Seeing how much Princess Angela missed her sister everyone tried their best to keep her happy.

Prince Robert was crowned as the new King one month after the death of Princess Maria. He was accepted by the citizens of his country in great jubilation. They were all glad that Prince Robert was their new King and not his brother.

Princess Rose was born a year after the coronation of her father, Prince Robert. During that year he had proved to everyone that he could run his country very efficiently. He was loved by everyone. Nobody suffered under his regime. The whole country celebrated at the birth of their Princess and hoped that she too would grow up to be just like her parents. Just as hoped, Princess Rose grew up to be loved by everyone. She was very kind and loving to them. She treated them as equals. She had a kind heart and couldn't bear to see anyone wronged or treated badly. She had heard about her uncle Prince Randall, about his treatment of others and the way her aunt Princess Maria, had died.

Not only was Princess Rose kind, loving, generous and forgiving but she was also very beautiful. She had long dark hair which reached down to her waist and beautiful grey-green eyes. She was the apple of her parents' and grandparents' eyes.

When Princess Rose was eighteen she received many proposals of marriage from princes all over the world. Many came to see her and proposed personally but she always refused, saying that she wasn't ready to marry yet and she would definitely know when her true love comes along.

It happened when she least expected it. Princess Rose was in the castle gardens picking flowers for her rooms with her maid. Her corgi, Spike, which had been given to her on her twentieth birthday the previous year, was playing nearby. She was looking forward to tomorrow. Her father was giving a big party for her twenty-first birthday. He had also declared a national holiday tomorrow. Princess Rose was so engrossed in picking the flowers that she did not hear Spike barking and a thud as someone fell to the ground. Her maid alerted her and when she turned around she saw what looked like a man sprawled on the ground and Spike licking his face. Princess Rose went to help the man up. She couldn't stop laughing at the scene before her. As she came nearer to the man she told Spike off mildly for being a nuisance and, still smiling, extended her hand to him to help him get up. At closer inspection she found that he was the most handsome man she had ever seen. She fell in love with him at first sight.

'Hello, what happened to you?' she said as she helped him up.

'My horse threw me when your dog barked at him. I believe he is your dog,' replied this stranger. Then, seeing the funny side of the situation, he too began to smile.

Princess Rose became utterly besotted by his smile. She'd never seen anyone so handsome and a smile so infectious, which changed his features completely. It felt as if the stars were shining out of his eyes.

'I haven't seen you here before. Can I help you?' asked Princess Rose.

'I am here to see King Robert concerning some business matters and also my father, King George, wants me to meet his daughter, Princess Rose. We have heard that until now she has refused to get married to anyone. She might refuse me. Is she as beautiful as they all say?'

'Yes, she is,' replied Princess Rose. For some reason

unknown to her she did not want to tell him that she was herself King Robert's daughter. Prince Harry thought to himself that no one could be as beautiful as this young woman before him. He had never believed in love at first sight but strangely he had definitely fallen in love with this woman.

'What's your name?' he asked.

Princess Rose thought quickly and said, 'Mary,' and quickly murmured something about having to take the flowers in and left Prince Harry standing there watching her go.

It's a pity I did not ask her anything about herself, but I will find out, thought Prince Harry. The way she was dressed shows she is of noble birth. It will not be hard to find out who she really is. Once I know, I am going to ask for her hand in marriage. Father expects me to marry this Princess Rose whom I have never seen. After seeing Mary there's no way I could marry anyone else, he said to himself as he saw Mary go back to pick up the basket full of flowers. Then he turned towards the castle and went in. The sooner he finished his business with King Robert the sooner he could find out more about Mary and go and see her. He could not wait until he saw her again.

Princess Rose went to her chambers to be met by her mother who informed her that they had a visitor who would be joining them for dinner. On hearing this she told her mother of the incident in the garden, leaving nothing out. Then she said shyly, 'Mother, he is the one for me. I am already in love with him.'

She told her mother not to say anything to Prince Harry or her father. When her mother left there was still an hour or so to go before dinner was served so Princess Rose took her time to get ready. Her heart told her that Prince Harry felt the same way about her as she did about him. Wouldn't he be surprised when he saw she was not the maid, as she had led him to believe, but the daughter of King Robert. She couldn't wait to see his face.

She was coming down the stairs in her favourite simple, yellow gown when she saw that her parents and Prince Harry were just making their way towards the dining room door.

Something made Prince Harry turn his attention towards the stairs. Before he could say anything, King Robert said, 'That's my daughter, Princess Rose.' As Princess Rose approached them Prince Harry could see that she was enjoying every minute of the situation and the way his look of utter surprise changed to recognition.

Well I never, he thought, at least I will not have to go and look for my love now, she is right here in front of me. If he was not mistaken, by the way she was looking at him he was sure she too had fallen in love with him.

After dinner, when Prince Harry found himself alone with King Robert, he asked King Robert for Princess Rose's hand in marriage. It was usual that when anyone asked for Princess Rose's hand in marriage, King Robert always called her over and asked her in front of the person concerned how she felt about it. He did the same now. In answer all Princess Rose did was to nod in affirmation, for all of a sudden she was too shy to speak in front of Prince Harry. She went back to her mother and told her, who told Prince Harry that her daughter would be delighted to marry him. The King and Queen decided that their engagement would be announced the next day as it was Princess Rose's birthday as well.

Princess Rose and Prince Harry were engaged the next day and Montania celebrated their engagement for a whole week instead of just one day.

A few days after Princess Rose's engagement to Prince Harry, Prince Randall turned up at the castle with a woman he said was his wife, called Princess Zelda. He had met her on one of his travels, married her and settled down to help her father run his country until her brother was old enough to run it himself which had happened a few years ago. Since then they both went on their travels to see different places and sights. Only two days ago they had heard about the engagement of Princess Rose so he told his wife that it was about time he went back to his country and tried to mend the rift between himself and his family.

Prince Randall told his father and brother how sorry he was for behaving the way he did and he hoped that they would forgive him and accept him and his wife back. He also told them that he didn't want to cause any trouble with anyone but all he wanted was to settle down in his country and amongst his family and help his brother with the running of the country.

Being of a forgiving nature, King Robert and his father forgave Prince Randall and welcomed both him and his wife, Princess Zelda, with open arms. Little did they know the tragedy which lay ahead for them all.

Once behind the closed doors of their living quarters, Prince Randall told his wife that he had been sure that he would have had to beg for their mercy into letting him back into Montania, let alone the castle, but now that he was in there was no way he was going to let anyone have what was rightfully his. First he would have to make them believe that he had changed and then strike.

He already had his men established in the castle. They had come with him when he had returned. He had told his brother, King Robert, that they always travelled with him wherever he went.

A week after his return to the castle Prince Randall and his men put their plan into action. Princess Zelda making a pretence of checking what was being served for dinner had gone down to the kitchen and, when no one was looking, had poured some kind of potion into the stew which was cooking in a big pot. At dinner no one noticed that Prince Randall and his wife were not eating the stew. Half an hour after dinner, everyone had fallen asleep in the parlour into which they had retired to have coffee or brandy. Prince Randall's men had already attacked the palace guards and killed them while they were having their dinner, so they were waiting just outside the parlour doors for Prince Randall's signal. He called them in and between them, they took King Robert and his family and Prince Harry into the dungeons. Prince Randall did not want Prince Harry involved in but couldn't help it as Prince Harry had arrived the day before to spend a few days with Princess Rose.

King Robert woke up with a heavy head. He felt very uncomfortable and cold. As realisation dawned, he became aware that he was in the dungeons. He wondered how he came to be there. The last thing he remembered was being in the parlour having a brandy with his family. He couldn't understand how he had come to be here. Slowly he looked around and was shocked to find that he was not alone. All his family were there with him except his brother Randall and his wife Princess Zelda. King Robert was so angry for now he realised that his brother must have been involved in them being there. He went to check how the others were. Slowly everyone woke up in utter disbelief.

'I knew that no-good son of mine was up to no good. We should never have accepted him back. Wait till I get my hands on him,' the former King said in an angry voice.

Before anyone could say anything the doors were opened to let in Prince Randall and his wife.

'Well, well, well, I see everyone is awake after their beautiful sleep,' he said as he came through the doors with his men. King Robert lunged forward to attack Prince Randall but was quickly pinned down by Prince Randall's men, as was everyone else.

'Why, Randall? Why did you do this? What have we

done to deserve this?' King Robert asked his brother.

'Don't you get it? Even now? I came back to take what was rightfully mine. You can't do anything now. My men have taken control of the castle. I was in exile for twenty-two years. Twenty-two long years. I have been waiting all that time for this minute, to see you all rot in hell,' said Prince Randall looking smug and pleased with himself with the turn of events.

'Oh, by the way,' he turned to his wife, brought her close to him and turned back again to face everyone and went on, 'there is something else I have to do, or rather my wife will do the good deed. You see, because of you lot I lost my first wife and my unborn child. You took my child from me; I will take yours from you.'

Saying this he turned to his wife who took out from the folds of the cape that she was wearing what looked like a black stick.

'By the way, I forgot to tell you my wife is a witch. When I left here all those years ago I had nowhere to go. I travelled all over the world taking on all kinds of manual labour to keep me alive. I was at my lowest when I met Zelda who took me in, looked after me and brought me back from death's door. We fell in love and got married. I told her everything and since then we have been waiting for the right moment. I see now my wait has been worthwhile.'

'Leave my daughter alone,' King Robert said angrily. 'It's me you want, not her.'

'Oh, I want you too, but I want you to suffer as I have suffered without my child. Zelda, do your stuff. I want everything over with so that I can settle down and rule the country.'

On Zelda's instructions the guards got hold of Princess Rose and took her away from the other to a secluded corner. Then Zelda waved her wand and turned Princess Rose into a glass rose. Seeing this, King Robert and Prince

Harry went to attack both Zelda and Prince Randall. Prince Randall's men were too strong for King Robert but somehow Prince Harry broke loose and went for Prince Randall but Prince Randall was ready for him and thrust his sword into Prince Harry's chest, killing him instantly.

'Take his body and dump it far away from here in the forest. The wild animals will finish him off,' Prince Randall told his men.

'Please bring my daughter back. We will leave the country, go away and will never come back,' King Robert begged his brother who just laughed at him and told him that from now on this is where they would stay and spend the rest of their lives. And now that Prince Harry is dead, nothing can bring his precious daughter back. For only her true love could do that. And even then only when he cut his finger and poured the blood on the rose willingly, would Princess Rose be brought back to life.

★

Ivan woke up with sweat pouring down his face and back. He turned the bedside lamp on to see the time. It was only two o'clock in the morning. He had been having these dreams since he was a child. When he first started having them he told his parents about them because it had frightened him. Ivan had also asked his parents about the significance of the dream but they could not tell him anything as they knew nothing about the kind of dreams Ivan was having. It was always the same dream. He was in a dark, cold place. There was hardly any light coming through the small opening in one wall. From somewhere in the cold place he could hear a woman's voice calling for help. No matter how much he searched around to see who was calling him, he could not see anything except a rose in one corner of the room. The voice seemed to come from somewhere around the rose. Just as he felt he was about to find who the caller was he would wake up. Every time the dream ended here. Even now it was the same. Ivan was wide awake and no matter how much he tried to relax and go back to sleep he could not. In the end he gave up trying to sleep and started thinking again about the dream. It must mean something otherwise he would not be getting these dreams. It seemed that someone was in trouble and needed his help but why him and why not anyone else? He could remember having them since he was five years old and now, even after twenty-five years he still had them. He decided that he had to do something about it or he would never be free of these dreams.

Once his mind was made up, Ivan got dressed, packed a few of his belongings and, as it was still early in the morning and he did not want to disturb his parents, he left them a note saying that he was going to be away for a while and not to worry about him and that he would be back as soon as possible. Ivan felt guilty about leaving his parents like this. He was their only child and, being farmers, he knew that he was leaving them in the lurch but he had to sort out the significance of his dreams. So, after leaving his parents' house, Ivan went straight to his friend John's house, woke him up, told him what he was about to do and asked John if he could help his parents while he was away.

'But where are you going?' John asked, still sleepy from his sleep and being woken up by Ivan in the middle of the night. 'What is so urgent that you have to leave in the middle of the night? Why can't you wait until morning and then go?'

'I might not have the courage to do what I want to do if I wait until morning. If I am to find any peace for myself, I have to go now,' Ivan told John who was very puzzled about why Ivan wanted to go away. Suddenly he remembered Ivan telling him about his recurring dreams.

'It's not something to do with your dreams, Ivan, is it?' John asked. 'You can't just leave everything and go and chase after those stupid dreams.'

'John, you'll never understand it but I believe someone is in trouble and needs my help,' Ivan said, trying to make his friend understand.

'But where will you go? You don't even know the place, or even who or what needs your help.' John persisted.

'I don't know the place, but all I know is that I will know the place when I see it. I don't even know how long I will be away. Please, John, look after my parents. They have no one else. Promise me you'll do that?' Ivan asked, emphasising the urgency of his last sentence.

'You know I will, Ivan. Just take care of yourself and come back soon,' John replied slowly. He knew he was going to miss his friend very much but he had to let his friend go for John knew from Ivan's previous talks with him how important it was to him to find the solution of his dreams.

Ivan left his friend at the gates of his house and went on his way to find something or someone who needed his help, to the unknown territory. He'd never before travelled more than ten miles or so from his farm so this was the first time he would be travelling far away. He was afraid of not knowing what lay ahead of him but he made up his mind and was very determined that nothing was going to stop him from finding out and solving the mystery of the dreams.

★

During the eight months of his travels Ivan had come upon many places and people all from different walks of life. When his money had run out he had taken any job that was going, made some more money and moved on. Quite a few times in the last few months he had nearly given up and decided to go back home, but he still had the dreams, and the next day he would carry on the search – but search for what, even he did not know. Only the voice of his dreams kept him going.

One sunny morning Ivan found himself walking down a huge mountain. He was deep in his own thoughts, wondering how quickly the last eight months had gone by. He had left his parents' farm in the middle of September and now it was the middle of May. The winter had been very harsh but he had always been lucky enough to find some sort of shelter, whether it was a barn or a small room which he would share with one of the family members if they were generous enough to take him in and give him a roof over his head.

Suddenly Ivan became aware of his surroundings. He felt as if he had been here before, but there were no landmarks or any houses here to indicate the location of the place. Only tall trees and wild flowers surrounded him. He went further down the mountain and suddenly he came out of the woods and into a clearing. The sight that greeted him was breathtaking. He could see three other mountains as high as the one he was on. All of them were covered with trees and as the leaves were just growing on most of them he could see bare spaces of ground between them and most of the space was covered with the bloom of wild flowers. Ivan felt so much at peace just looking at the sight that greeted him. He allowed his gaze to travel to the bottom of the valley in between the mountains. He just stood transfixed for below him in the valley stood a castle which was surrounded by a moat, and beyond that he could see houses all around the castle. He felt that he had been here before. The surroundings were very familiar to him. Ivan quickened his pace. He knew in his heart that he had reached his destination at last.

As Ivan approached the houses his awareness of the familiarity of the place increased. He knew that he should be heading towards the castle but something held him back. A few yards away Ivan saw a church so he went towards it and went inside and sat down on the front pew. He couldn't understand why he was frightened to go into the castle. He was still deep in thought when a priest came in from the side entrance. He was surprised to see a new face in the church. He hadn't seen any new faces for the past twenty years or so, not since Prince Randall had overthrown his brother, King Robert, and taken over as the new King. He had insisted on everyone calling him King Randall. Since his becoming king, Montania had gone downhill. It was nearly in ruins now. Montania's citizens were all robbed of their worldly goods and left to work for King Randall alone. Seventy per cent of their produce and cattle had to be given to the King every year and the citizens were left to survive on whatever was left over. Any outsiders who came here were either turned away or they disappeared for good. Everyone feared the wrath of the King and his witch wife. If anyone went against their wishes they were made to suffer by her casting spells on them, so everyone feared them.

The priest thought how good it was to see a new face here but that he must warn this young man and tell him to leave as soon as possible. As he approached the young man something clicked in his mind and it felt as if it was only yesterday when King Robert and Queen Angela had come here with their daughter and her fiancé for the blessing. He tried to recall the name of the fiancé and suddenly came quite close and said 'Prince Harry, is that you? Of course it is you. I am very good with faces. How could I forget your face? Do you remember you were here with Princess Rose? But how can it be? You still look the same. But that was twenty-five years ago!'

Ivan became aware of someone talking to him. He looked up to the person who was talking to him and realised that it was a priest. He only caught the last part of the sentence.

'I'm sorry, Father, can you say that again? I'm sorry, I was not listening to you properly,' Ivan asked the priest, so the priest repeated to Ivan what he had said earlier.

'I'm not Prince Harry, Father. My name is Ivan.'

'But you look so much like Prince Harry.'

'Who is this Prince Harry, Father?' asked Ivan.

The priest told Ivan everything, from the former King, Prince Robert's coming to the throne, Princess Rose's engagement to Prince Harry, the arrival of Prince Randall and the disappearance of the rest of the royal family since his arrival, to the subsequent decline of the country and how no outsiders were allowed to come here.

'I am surprised you got here without anyone seeing you, especially the guards. They would have killed you because of your resemblance to Prince Harry,' finished the priest.

Ivan told the priest about the dream, how he had set out to solve the mystery, how familiar this place was to him and also about how he felt frightened of going to the castle, and had therefore ended up here in the church instead.

'I don't know whether you believe me or not,' said the priest, 'but I reckon you are Prince Harry reincarnated because you look exactly like him. And in your dreams, I feel King Robert and the rest of his family are still alive and are locked up somewhere.'

All this talk about Prince Harry and his likeness to him was frightening Ivan but he had come this far and there was no way he was going to back away. 'Father, do you know anyone you can trust who works in the castle?' asked Ivan.

The priest said that he did. There was a woman who worked in the kitchen of the castle. He said he would go and see her that evening, and told Ivan that he could stay in the church. He also told Ivan not to venture out at all. He showed Ivan his private quarters above the church and left him there promising to be back by the evening, and went away.

It was nearly ten o'clock when the priest came back. Ivan was very eager to hear what he had to say. There was someone else with the priest, an old woman. She looked at Ivan and said, 'Oh my God, you are right,' and just stared at Ivan. The priest introduced her as the cook and said that she had been at the castle as cook all her life. Ivan managed to find out the layout of the castle, and asked her to describe every room in it. None of them came close to what he had seen in his dreams. He asked the cook if she remembered any cold, dark room with a small round window or some kind of opening in one wall. After some thought she replied, 'What you are describing sounds like the dungeons, but no one goes there. I used to go with a maid to clean up, but that was nearly thirty years ago. The doors are padlocked and guarded.'

'So they are all in the dungeons,' said the priest excitedly. 'I hope they are still alive.'

'I feel it in my bones. They are still alive,' replied Ivan.

'Oh dear, I have been there all this time and not even realised that they were all there. Oh, just the thought of those poor souls, suffering,' cried the cook and burst out crying.

The priest talked to her in soothing tones. When she had quietened down he made her promise not to say anything about their talk to anyone for if the other royals were still alive and shut up in the dungeons then their lives might be in danger. Ivan asked the priest if he knew anyone who would be willing to help him get into the castle and rescue the prisoners.

'I will ask around discreetly and get back to you,' he replied and left him to rest, saying he would see him the next day.

By the end of the week, at around half past eleven in the evening, the church was full of people who were willing to help Ivan get into the castle and overthrow Prince Randall and his army. Most of the older generation were very surprised to see Ivan and his likeness to Prince Harry. All the citizens were very unhappy and they wanted their King, King Robert, back on the throne.

Even then it took another week to arrange everything and to finalise their plans very carefully. Ivan had suggested that they make Prince Randall and his army weak by drugging them all, and the only way it could be done was to put sleeping potion in everyone's meal. He couldn't figure out for himself why he had said what he did about drugging Prince Randall and his army but he felt that it was the right way to go about it. Everybody agreed with him as well and so it was decided that they would attack the castle the following day in the evening at around nine o'clock, the reason being that everyone had their meal at around eight o'clock and by the time they entered the castle Prince Randall and his men would be fast asleep.

That night Ivan had the same dream again. This time he could see everything clearly. He recognised the former King and Queen, King Robert and Queen Angela. He also saw Princess Zelda with a wand in her hand and Prince Randall beside her. He tried to see where Princess Rose was but could not see. Instead in her place was a glass rose. He tried to break free but could not.

The priest heard noises coming from the room next to his. He quickly went there and saw by the moonlight which was filtering through the windows that Ivan was tossing and turning in the bed and calling out Princess Rose's name. He knew that Ivan was having a nightmare so he gently started shaking Ivan and woke him up.

'You were having a bad dream,' said the priest and gave

Ivan a glass of water. After drinking the water and wiping the sweat from his face Ivan told the priest about his dream and that it was the first time he could see everyone's faces and recognise them as well, and also that he saw everyone except Princess Rose. Then he described everyone to the priest who told Ivan that indeed they were the right people:

'Whether you believe me now or not you are indeed Prince Harry and your dreams have brought you here to release all of them.'

Then he told Ivan to sleep because the next day was going to be a long day for everyone. To his surprise Ivan did fall asleep and woke the next day very relaxed.

At the appointed time, Ivan entered the castle with the citizens of Montania. Everyone knew what they had to do. Ivan went straight to the parlour. In the parlour he found Prince Randall and Princess Zelda fast asleep. With others' help he tied their wrists and took them and the sleeping men to the dungeons. After locking them up separately, Prince Randall and Princess Zelda in one room, he went in search of the former King and Queen, King Robert, Queen Angela and his beloved Rose. There were many rooms to go through. In the end he came upon one room which was padlocked. Breaking the padlock, Ivan went in. The sight which greeted him was pitiful. In one corner on a makeshift bed, a blanket covered two figures. On the other side just below the small window which Ivan had seen in his dreams, were two small beds. Someone was lying on each of them.

With his half-closed eyes, King Robert saw someone approaching him with a burning torch. He thought that Randall was coming to gloat and laugh at him so he just stayed where he was and waited for Randall to come near, and utter his abuse and leave. By now he was too weak to answer back. It wouldn't be long before he too joined his father and mother in heaven. At the moment Angela was very weak and he doubted that she would last another week. As Randall approached, King Robert realised that it was not Randall but someone else looking down on him. He jumped up from the bed and nearly fell down on the floor in his weakened state and whispered, 'It can't be. You are dead. I saw them kill you and take your body out of here.'

'Who are you talking about?' Ivan asked.

'Prince Harry, of course,' replied King Robert.

'I have come back to save you all, King Robert.'

'It's a dream. This cannot be happening. I am having a dream, or have you come back as an angel to take me and Angela with you?' asked King Robert disbelievingly.

'No, it's not a dream, I am real. See, touch me.' Saying this Ivan sat down beside King Robert.

King Robert was so happy that in between crying and laughing he just hugged Ivan very tightly as if Ivan was a lifeline which if he let go would disappear. Gently Ivan soothed King Robert. By now Queen Angela was wide awake and, with tears streaming down her face, she approached Ivan slowly and hugged him. All three of them sat there for what seemed like hours but which was only for a few minutes. Ivan asked if they should wake the former King and Queen only to be told that they were dead. No wonder the air in here smelt so foul. By the look of his beard King Robert had not shaved for a good few years and had aged a great deal. He looks very old compared to what I remember from my dream, thought Ivan.

Then he went to the door and shouted to the others for help. In no time at all the priest entered the room with a few men. They all had tears in their eyes at the scene which greeted them.

All of a sudden Ivan asked King Robert about Princess Rose. King Robert's face fell again and he went back to the top of the bed and slowly took a small packet out from beneath it. Whatever it was, it was wrapped up in a very old shawl. Slowly King Robert unwrapped the shawl and took a glass rose out of it. Ivan realised it was the same rose he had seen in his dreams. He gently took it in his hands and just stared at it with tears streaming down his face. King Robert told them what Zelda had done to his beautiful daughter.

'Is there anything that can be done to bring her back?' asked Ivan.

'No,' replied King Robert, then suddenly he looked at Ivan and said, 'Wait, only her true love could do that. Even though they killed Prince Harry, you came back to save us all. If anyone can bring her back it could only be her true love. Ivan, I believe it to be you. Only you can bring her back. Will you do what you have to do to get my daughter back?'

'What do I have to do? Just tell me and I will do it,' replied Ivan, now very eager to see his beloved Rose again.

'You have willingly to cut your finger and let the blood trickle on the rose. Only then will my daughter be back to her normal self.'

'Then what are we waiting for?' Saying this, Ivan took the priest's blessing and put the glass rose in the middle of the bed. Then he stood over it and, holding his finger out, cut it with a sword. Slowly the blood from the cut finger started to trickle over the rose. Soon it was covered in Ivan's blood, and then a miracle happened. Right before their eyes the glass rose changed into Princess Rose. No one could believe their eyes.

Princess Rose opened her eyes. The first person she saw was her beloved Prince Harry. She went straight into his arms. Then she saw her parents and went to them to be embraced by both of them. King Robert asked Ivan where his brother and his wife the witch were. They were then all taken to the room where Prince Randall and Zelda were locked up. After opening the door, King Robert went in to find his brother and Zelda in chains. Both their hands were chained and secured to the wall on either side of them. Prince Randall was wide awake and trying his best to get out of the chains.

'Well, well, well,' said King Robert, 'I see that the tables have turned, Brother. I trusted you once and what did you do? You locked us all up for twenty-five years.'

'You are free, Robert, but your daughter will never be free. You will still suffer from the loss,' Prince Randall sniggered.

'You are wrong there again.'

As he said this King Robert beckoned Princess Rose and Ivan to come forwards. Prince Randall could not believe it. It could not be true. He himself had killed Prince Harry and had him thrown into the mountains.

'You see I have come back again to take my revenge,' Ivan told Prince Randall.

Locking the door again they all went back to the castle. Word had already gone around about King Robert being back on the throne. Montania was in full swing with celebrations.

The next day, the former King and Queen were buried in the royal cemetery. All the citizens turned up at the funeral.

An announcement was made that the beheading of Prince Randall and Zelda would take place the following day. This time quite a large crowd gathered to see the beheading of Prince Randall and Zelda. Word had got around to other countries as well and they all came to see the execution.

Prince Harry's father, King George, also came. He had received a message from King Robert about the 'rebirth' of Prince Harry who was very eager to meet King George. King George also wanted to meet his son who had come back from the dead. Up until now he had wondered what had happened to his son who had disappeared suddenly without any trace. King Robert had explained everything in his message to King George.

The priest had told King Robert that as Zelda was a witch it would be better to burn her body after the execution so that she would not come back again. Her wand was already destroyed by Ivan on the night of their capture so after the execution of Prince Randall and Zelda, they were both burned.

At last Montania was a happy place again. On instructions from King Robert, Ivan had called his parents over to the castle. He had already met King George and had immediately recognised him as his father from his previous life.

Princess Rose and Ivan were married a fortnight after the execution and they all lived happily ever after in Montania.